A Year in Ink

VOLUME 4

A Year in Ink

SAN DIEGO WRITERS, INK
ANTHOLOGY
VOLUME 4

Edited by Jericho Brown and Laurel Corona

THE
INK SPOT
PRESS
San Diego, California

A Year in Ink is a publication of
Ink Spot Press
San Diego Writers, Ink
PO Box 34374
San Diego, CA 92163

Editorial Committee: Jackie Bouchard, Kirsten Kessler,
                          Donna Marganella, Judy Reeves,
                          Kelli Wescott

Cover art: Setting Free the Collection
©2003 Kirsten Francis

Design and typography: Armadillo Creative

ISBN 978-0-9799204-4-8

Printed in the United States of America
Printed by Lightning Source Inc.

Contents

The Conversation

I am a poet because I take way too much too seriously. Even when I was really young I was excited about sentences. I remember being a kid in elementary school and knowing the difference between a comma and a semicolon and my teacher being proud of me because of that. I liked the feeling her pride gave me. For me and for the poets in this anthology, the semicolon is real business.

Commas and dashes and colons and exclamation points and question marks are really very important to us when it comes to how the poem is going to be read aloud, and what's going to happen for readers when they read the poem. You know you're a poet when you type an em dash and you hit the delete button, and you type a colon, and you hit the delete button, and you type an em dash and you hit the delete button, and you type a colon and you hit the delete button. If you can wrack your brain trying to figure which is the best one, if you can do that for three hours straight and call it a good time, then you're probably a poet.

I've always been taken with the idea that anything you do, you have to do completely and all the way. That's how you stake a place for yourself as a writer. Now when I say "for yourself as a writer" I don't mean in this in a competitive way. I mean you have to become aware of what your talents are, and you have to milk them for everything they're worth, and you have to become aware of where you're weak, and you have to try and strengthen that as best you can.

At the end of this labor, there is the poem—music made out of a combination of words. Poets manipulate words into this music. That's our job. But do not be mistaken. Poems don't just make music. They make meaning as well. And a line break is a moment of doubt, a doubt that feels more intense than suspense. Poetry is different from prose because it is infused with doubt. At the moment of a line break, even if it's for a millisecond, you're thrust into doubt, you're thrust into a place where you're not certain what just happened or what's going to happen. In that millisecond, you are plunged into a moment of rupture.

Let me go a step further in case I've mischaracterized my notion of meaning. Because they are full of doubt, poems ask us not to understand. Yes, it hurts. Poems do carry meaning, but their meaning should not be what attracts us to them. I've never believed what attracts us to poems is knowing what's going on in poems. As a matter of fact, I think just the opposite. Oh, I do want poems to have meaning, but I also know that meaning isn't the end of the conversation. I hope the poems in this book are the beginning of the conversation.

Jericho Brown

Introduction

I love words. I love their shapes and sounds, and how we can use them to make meaning. Though as a novelist, I'm usually wrapped up in what I'm doing personally with these squiggly and slashy little creatures. When I was asked to be the prose editor for the 2011 San Diego Writers, Ink Anthology, I thought it would be fun to see what other people are putting on the page.

Some of the entries I read went places I didn't much like going—into violence, despair, and deep, deep loss. I rode in a car while a young woman is taken to a psychiatric hospital, explored with a grieving son the last home of his estranged father, hung by the wrists in a basement while friends were being murdered upstairs, went on a desert hike with a troubled but vibrant young woman and witnessed a blood-coated father trying to help his suicidal son. Others entries took me on joy rides with some hilarious, quirky people. I went through the first weeks of a new school with an outcast seventh grader, spent an afternoon in a car with a most engaging uncle and tried to get myself out a too-small bag I had been talked into wiggling into on a dare.

Making the final choices for this anthology was difficult, for less than 20 percent of the submissions could be included. Some of the authors made it easy. Some pieces were polished and well edited, ringing with excellent, musical phrasing and just-right word choices. They were exactly the right length, whether 200 or 2000 words. No wasted energy, no wasted words. It didn't matter to me at that point whether I liked the subject matter or the characters. Good writing is good writing.

On the other hand, some pieces were works in progress not yet ready for publication. Some were not economical enough with language, or didn't have a clear voice or narrative point of view. Some told rather than showed, or hadn't been thoroughly edited for grammar and mechanics. I had difficulty with pieces that were excerpted from novels, because despite being well written (and I wish their authors well in that genre), novels are paced, populated and structured differently and the excerpts did not stand alone very successfully. On the other hand, many pieces would have benefited from a few more drafts, or read-and-critique workshopping, or just a thorough editing before submission. I encourage anyone whose piece was not selected to keep working on it, but unfortunately, when submissions had to be whittled down to a few, I had to go with the ones that were ready to be published as they were.

As a writer myself, I've learned the point at which I first think a piece is done, I am probably less than two-thirds there. Editing is exhausting. I find it much harder than drafting, but there is no substitute for creating a finished product by layering it, revision by revision, until everything is as good as you can make it. Then, you put it aside, because you still aren't done. Later you will be able to improve it more. The hard part is even after it's published you would have been able to make it better still. Those looking at their first published work in this anthology have probably just learned that, like the rest of us, they will have to live with the winces, groans, and awareness of missed opportunities that are part of seeing one's work on the printed page.

I'm very proud to be part of the San Diego writing community. We have renowned programs at local universities, and my own institution, San Diego City College, is home to City Works Press, which publishes the annual City Works Journal and excellent books by local authors. The Ink Spot serves for many as the locus for writing and writers in our community, and with the overall high quality and range of the submissions for this anthology, it seems clear that San Diego is continuing to grow as one of the best places for writers to be. With that, I invite you to lose yourself in some of the finest writing by local authors in the last year.

Laurel Corona

Blessing

Lisa Grove

May you snow.

May Aeolus carve canyons across your body. May he shape you
into arches and hoodoos.

May he wear you away. Each day may you be worn down more,
until you are dust.

May the whims of his winds loose you from the limits your feet
once knew

and bring you more comfort than the couch of your study ever
could.

Go, and as a grain over Everest, may you grow heavy
with the bonds of hydrogen and oxygen.

Go, and as you linger above a quilted landscape, I pray that your
cheekbones crystallize

and drift down onto noses and tongues, daring each other to
stick further out.

Noses and tongues, admiring the hexagonal perfection
of your existence as it melts away
on mittens, in the brief warmth of human breath.

Grey Wash of Rain

Nicole Vollrath

When your heart shatters, stillness becomes a danger. Beware of gravity slugging your body to the couch, leeching you deep into chairs, seducing you with the prospect of immobility. Refuse the relief of becoming a salt-scarred anchor, defeated by the weight of the sea. Death is not an option. Keep moving.

Tune your nose like a Setter's and hunt for a sky that is a grey wash of rain. Seek a city of stone-faced buildings, weary and pocked. A place that has seen hunger and loss. Warsaw. Prague. Moscow in its fifth month of winter.

Traverse desolate landscape on slow-moving trains, lumbering iron beasts on which you feel every bump-and-sway like a saddle sore. The window will be cold to the touch. Newspapers, meaningless. The horizon, a blank head of steam.

The train station smells of onion and ice. Fingers shrink in their gloves and snow pricks your face like razor burn. In the square, talk is muffled by scarves, clipped by frost, guttural grunts rationed out like turnips in a Gulag.

His name is a note on an underground violin played over and over and over, regular as breath.

Walk until your toes have numbed; until your boots stumble over cobblestone curbs. Inhale the grit, the rusting trash, of every foreign street. Crows mock you from bare trees. Walk until your knees groan, your ass aches, your calves moan from miles logged. There are never enough miles between How You Were and Who You Are, between Being Loved and Now.

The restaurant should have tablecloths, linen napkins, heavy forks. A menu in a leather folder offered by a waiter whose apron rises to his armpits. His face remains impassive when you dismiss the wine list with a word: cognac. Unwind your scarf. Let your limbs thaw. Order stroganoff and take a lifetime eating it; winding each noodle around your fork; pricking each perfect, wine-soaked mushroom; chewing beef with the relief of an abandoned dog.

Test the building blocks of basic feeling: hot, cold, empty, warm. Test your tolerance for company.

Though the restaurant gets crowded, keep the empty chair across from you. It is a place your grief can occupy, a seat where she can stretch, tall and wide as a cemetery angel, marble wings aloft. Conversation is not needed. She is all there is to say.

how the wounded dream speaks

Carrie Moniz

we love the moon alive. the rain
out of exile. Saguaros line up to bless us
against each wild strike of lightning. cloudbursts
ravage the earth's old body. she relishes the force.
The quick flooding of dry beds.

we drink to the flood. we drink.
we drink to salt. to hands. my body
gnawed as a cage. I dance
and you chant. your voice a bird sky.
when not the journey I am stone.
when not stone I am the valley.
how I bear the land. granite. sediment. dying. moss.
I know that ache. pages of bone. faults.

we hike the peaks speaking soil and stars.
your tongue. I want to know every inch.
desert and moon-bound. we haul the road behind us.
our shadows, dark scars across our path.

even our laughter is filled with ghosts. each breath.
I wake in a valley of sage like an answer.
the clouds were water and will be again.
I can only speak fire. your body blazing. these days
are heavy on my back. beneath my sheets
a mountain is burned clean.

we answered the call. split our bodies into wind.
now, I walk this road. barefoot. throat closed with dust.
I write the ghosts. I write the moss.

Canyon Girl

Cris Powell

"We do, doodley do, doodley do, doodley do,
what we must, muddily must, muddily must, muddily must..."
— BOKONON

I'm walking through a desert canyon with a pair of Wiccans, about to perform a ritual in the middle of my work day. Hot, brittle brush crunches under our sandals. Crows caw from bare tree branches as we pass.

What's a nice Christian girl like me doing in a scene like this?

Rhiannon came to Canyon Ridge for long-term residential treatment after she slit her wrists. She'd been carving on her arms since she was twelve but now, at fifteen, she cut deeper.

Ry's mother would not allow her to return home until she saw radical change in her attitude and behavior. The two together were gasoline and flame. Their violent fights had resulted in two evictions, and their new landlord now threatened a third.

The group home staff called Ry *cold-hearted* and claimed she had no empathy. When one of her peers almost died from a suicide attempt, Ry laughed at her.

I liked Ry. I saw a softness in her. Under her baggy men's XL shirts, she wore frilly cotton dresses. She reminded me of those little monster finger puppets with the huge buggy eyes that look more scared than scary. For ten years I'd worked as a therapist with severely emotionally disturbed adolescents. I moseyed around the group home campus in long, flowing therapist skirts and Doc Martens, humming a happy tune. Helping kids was my dream. During Ry's first six months of residential treatment, her mom refused to take her on passes. She wanted to punish her, and she also wanted to keep her safe.

Susan, a tough, practical woman, did not understand her sensitive, artistic daughter. Susan had grown up with a psychotic mother, and dropped out of school at sixteen to work. She wanted to give Ry a better life, and she worked hard to be a good provider.

Ry adored her dad, and blamed Susan for driving him away. Dad called Ry every week, badmouthed Susan, and sent frivolous gifts. He never paid a dime of child support.

Susan agreed to participate in family therapy sessions every other Friday after work. She drove her truck over an hour in heavy traffic and arrived early for our first session.

She sat on the couch; arms folded, jaws tight, and watched Ry with suspicion.

Ry pleaded with her mother. "Give me another chance! Pleease!" Tears streamed down her face. "I want to come home."

"Don't give me your crocodile tears," Susan snapped. "We've been through this too many times before. You cry and say you're sorry, and then you go out and do the same things."

"But, Mom..."

"I can't believe anything she says anymore," Susan told me. "She's a compulsive liar."

"She left me all alone!" Ry wailed, "What was I supposed to do?"

"Well, maybe you could take some responsibility for helping out around the house instead of carving yourself up and running off with hoodlums," Susan said.

"She won't let me do anything," Ry said. "She treats me like a prisoner."

"You mean I grounded you for running away and doing crystal?" Susan confronted her. "Why don't you tell Dr. Powell about your little tantrum?."

Ry slouched into the sofa and folded her arms across her chest.

"I came home from work late one night, and she started screaming at me, called me a cunt, and broke two of the dining room chairs," Susan said. "The next day, she shaved her head and pierced her nose while I was at work."

"Well you leave me all alone in that fuckin' apartment," Ry yelled. "You act like you don't even care about me."

Susan rolled her eyes and looked at me. "Drama," she said, and shook her head.

The accumulated pain and rage between them seemed endless. Neither could empathize with the other's perspective. Both wanted revenge.

Susan could not empathize with Ry because her mother had never empathized with her. And Ry was desperate for a little empathy.

We met twice a month, and I searched for some point of connection. Susan seemed hard. Ry told me her mom was totally shut down. It was hard to discern how much of Susan's armor was in response to Ry's abuse.

Ry, on the other hand, was a wound that wouldn't stop bleeding.

I talked to Susan on the phone between sessions and tried to form an alliance. I told her about Ry's progress in the program. One of her treatment goals was to communicate directly instead of manipulating. It was a tough habit to break, but she did it.

Ry worked hard to regain her mother's trust. I tried to mediate.

Problem was Susan didn't trust therapists any more than she trusted Ry. They always blamed the mother.

After a few months of family therapy, I didn't feel much hope of connecting with Susan, and I worried that Ry would not be able to return home.

Meanwhile, my own happy home had broken up when my roommate fell in love with a woman at work and went off to make turkey baster babies.

I moved to a secluded cottage in the middle of a vineyard, and embarked upon a relationship with *Sensitive Pony Tail Man,* who brought me long-stemmed roses and took me touring through forest-lined mountain roads on his sexy Italian motorcycle.

It felt so weird to be somebody's girlfriend after eight years of marriage/divorce and another five years of *Will I Ever Recover From That Train Wreck?* The first time we went out to dinner, I practically had a panic attack. You might say I was skittish.

My new boyfriend was a therapist, and he said all the right things. He prepared candle-lit dinners, and wrote songs for me, which he played on my guitar when he came to visit.

But, after six months of motorcycle riding, Pony Tail abruptly morphed into *Unspeakable Lying Bastard* and ran off with an older, blonder woman who had a prison record. She wore a leopard print mini-dress to the Canyon Ridge Christmas party.

Therapists are crazy. Don't ever date one.

One afternoon Ry stomped into my office wearing her dad's brown work boots, plopped down on the couch, and downloaded her weekend on the dorm. She had taken on Maggie, supervisor of the girls' dorm, in a battle for religious freedom.

No one challenges Mag.

Ry loved witchcraft. While the other girls kept bibles on their night tables, Ry kept her spell books and tarot cards.

An angry Maggie knocked on my door that evening.

"She's scarin' those girls with all that satanic stuff!" Maggie squawked through vocal chords that had been ravaged by years of smoking and drinking. " They have a hard enough time feelin' safe on that dorm without her puttin' spells on 'em!"

I motioned for Mag to sit, and let her vent her spleen.

"I confiscated all that stuff and put it in a box," Mag said. "You can give it to her mother when she comes on Friday."

She ranted awhile longer and then calmed down. "I'll bring that stuff over here at the end of my shift," she said as she walked out.

I adored Maggie. She had the crustiest crust and the biggest heart to go with it. She was harder on the girls than the rest of us, but she would have given her life for any one of them.

Now, the thing about Canyon Ridge: it was staffed primarily by fundamentalist Christians who all attended the same mega church a few miles up the road.

Ry's magical paraphernalia might as well have been concealed weapons.

That evening Mag brought the box to me and told me more about her ongoing war with Ry.

After she left, I opened up the box. I recognized the *Dream Catcher* that used to dangle above Ry's pillow, and her collection of crystals that she kept in a bowl on her nightstand.

I picked up Ry's spell book and leafed through it. It looked like a recipe book with elegant sketches and quotations. Bookmarks stuck out in three places.

I read the titles of the three spells she'd marked. *Breaking A Bad Habit. Forgiving a Wrong. Letting Go Of Resentments.*

Funny...that's the same language Mag uses in her 12-Step Group.

I looked around my office at the dense crowd of sand tray miniatures and symbols that filled the shelves. The wicked witch of the West sat next to Glenda, good witch of the East. Jewish symbols sat beside the Virgin Mary, St. Francis, Shiva, and Buddha. Crosses and dream catchers shared the same basket with sage and crystals.

In the world of expressive arts therapies, no one is excluded.

The next day, Ry came to me with a proposition.

"Can I keep my spell book and tarot cards in your office?" She put on her sweetest puppy dog face, cocked her head to the side and batted her long lashes.

Then she brought out the big guns: the dimples.

"We can play with them in session!" she bounced on the couch, eyes sparkling with anticipation.

I swallowed.

I agreed with Ry that she had just as much right to practice her religion as the other girls, but the group home rules were clear: no witchcraft, no Wicca, no magic.

"I'll think about it," I said.

She smiled triumphantly.

Little shit.

What if she tells Mag?

I'm supposed to return this stuff to her mother.

Who is she putting spells on anyway?

Ry trotted back to the dorm. I sat and pondered.

I conjured my open-minded colleagues: Lali's adventures with the shamans, Ingrid's charismatic priest who cast out bad spirits, and Kate, whose cancer disappeared after she saw a spiritual healer in Bali.

I thought about Barb's women's group, which her boyfriend liked to call *The Coven*. They were like family. Yeah, they played with tarot cards and astrological charts, but they were so supportive of Barb. I remembered the day she came to work with rose petals all over her Rav 4. The Coven did a ritual to bless her new car. She was so happy.

I hid Ry's spell book and tarot cards in the bottom drawer of my desk, and we made them part of our work together. Ry became much more enthusiastic about therapy.

She told me about her beliefs. She didn't want to do any harm with her magic, but she thought she could do some healing.

Ry poured out her pain. She felt abandoned and terrified at home when her mom worked late. She carved on her arms out of desperation.

She told me all the horrible things they had said to each other in anger, the objects they'd thrown and broken. Ry couldn't remember ever having fun with her mom, who seemed humorless and unreachable. She longed to live with her dad in New Mexico. When mom said "no," Ry ran away for several days.

As Ry told her story and cried week after week, her rage quieted down. She gained better control over her emotions.

Mischief replaced her dark brooding, and she bonded with her peers. They started getting in trouble for playing pranks instead of abusing the staff.

She stopped carving on her arms, and applied cocoa butter to her scars.

One Friday before family session, Mag called me from the dorm. "Ry wants to talk to you before her mom gets here," she said.

"O.K. Bring her over."

A few minutes later, Mag knocked on my door. "What's up?" I asked Ry. Mag stood beside her. I suddenly felt nervous.

"Can I come in?" Ry asked. She looked nervous too.

"Sure."

I nodded to Mag and she walked back to the dorm.

Ry closed the door.

"I want to tell my mom about Wicca," she said. "I think she'll like it."

"Really?"

"Yeah. She used to have a spell book a long time ago." Ry looked away, wistful. "I think it will help us." She looked at me. "Can we show her the spell book in session?"

Susan and Ry sat side by side on the sofa, as usual. These sessions were always painful, and I dreaded them

"Cris, can I show my mom my spell book?"

I opened the desk drawer and handed her the book.

Susan looked at me, surprised. The veil dropped from her eyes for the first time.

Ry scooted over closer to her mom and showed her the book. She spoke with the soft voice of a young child. Susan seemed interested, attentive. Huddled side-by-side on the sofa, they looked like they were reading a bedtime story together.

After that, when the other girls asked to go to the taco shop, Ry wanted to go to the metaphysical bookstore. She worked hard in the treatment program and earned day passes to go out to lunch with her mom.

One Monday morning when I arrived at work, Ry was lurking in the hall, eager to tell me about her pass with her mom on the weekend.

Her mom had taken her to the metaphysical bookstore where they shopped for rocks, crystals, and goodies for magic potions. She showed me a chunk of rose quartz her mom had given her.

Mother and daughter were playing together for the first time.

After a few more weeks, Ry earned her first overnight pass. Maggie reminded her of the rules, and of the consequences for rule breaks. We crossed our fingers and sent her off with mom, hoping she would use the new skills we'd taught her.

The following Monday, Ry looked like a new girl. Her black eye liner and dark lipstick were gone. Her fresh scrubbed freckles pooched out above her dimpled grin. Instead of black jeans and baggy flannel, she wore a blouse she had borrowed from her mom.

"My mom bought me a new spell book!" she told me. "We're going to share it."

"You look happy," I said.

"And we went to the craft store and got some stuff to decorate the apartment!" She bounced up and down in her pink sneakers.

That afternoon, Susan called. During the weekend, Ry had told her about the religious discrimination on the dorm.

"This is our family's religion," Susan said. "Ry has just as much right to have her spell book as those girls do their bibles."

When I told Ry about my conversation with her mom, she swooned like she was in love.

When Susan arrived for family session on Friday, she confronted Maggie and demanded that Ry be allowed to keep her religious paraphernalia in her room. She had no luck obtaining equal rights for her daughter, but she became Ry's hero in front of all the other girls on the dorm.

I felt a little duplicitous that evening when Mag stopped by my office to vent about "the crazy lady with the witchcraft."

Oh well. What she doesn't know won't hurt her.

The energy Ry once spent fighting now flowed into projects that she shared with her mom. The pair spent their weekends shopping for magical rocks and making crafts together. They became friends.

On a Monday afternoon, after another successful weekend with mom, Ry came to my office with a protruding shirt pocket. She pulled out a wad of cloth, and reverently unwrapped a chunk of deep purple amethyst.

"I found the perfect ritual for me and my mom," she said. "It's a fire ritual."

"Fire is supposed to be heavy magic," I said.

"Yeah!" she smiled, happy that I remembered. Ry explained the ritual. She wanted to perform it during a family session with her mom, and she wanted it to be a surprise.

But, matches and mojos are not allowed in good Christian group homes.

We were going to have to sneak.

I remembered the time when a wise mentor told me, "Maybe you're too open-minded."

Nah.

This kid had found magic to heal her family that none of us could conjure.

We were going to the canyon.

Ry knew that my spiritual beliefs were different from hers, and that made my support more precious to her.

I didn't really believe that her spells were supernatural, but if she believed it, it would probably work.

To me, her rituals looked like expressive art therapy.

I helped Ry smuggle her ingredients into my office bit by bit, until she had everything she needed for her ritual. I would provide the fire.

On the first Friday after the full moon, Ry prepared her spell.

She spread a cloth on my office floor and crushed up dried sage and lavender. She added a cup of coarse salt and mixed them all together. Then she sprinkled a few drops of sandalwood oil on top and tied it all up in a bundle.

Ry reached into her shirt pocket and pulled out a crumpled piece of paper. "These are all my resentments," she said. "We're going to burn them in the fire."

"That is very cool," I nodded.

Ry packed her treasures into her backpack just as her mom knocked on the door. The three of us sneaked out the back and walked down a dusty road toward the canyon.

We hiked through the grey, crispy desert under the summer sun, past fragrant sage bushes, and out of view of Canyon Ridge.

Ry spotted a perfect place to make a fire. Susan and I gathered twigs while Ry built a small altar of stones in the dry stream bed, laying twigs on top of her magical bundle, and shoving the crumpled list of resentments under the twigs.

I handed her a book of matches, and she made a fire.

The aroma of lavender and sage rose up in the heat. I watched the smoke rise, and wondered if anyone could see it from the group home.

While the fire burned, Ry read her spell aloud.

All hatred and bitterness be gone
Leave me when the fire is done
Fire burn to remove all ill
By the power of my will

We watched the list of resentments shrink to ash. Dried leaves hissed and crackled in the flames.

"Now let us make a circle and join hands," Ry said.

We stood in a circle holding hands until the fire died.

Ry uttered the magic words, "I forgive."

She released our hands, unwrapped the purple stone, and clasped it tightly between her palms.

"Into this stone I put all my anger and all of my mistakes from the past," she said. "I cast it away and it is gone forever."

She held her mother in a solemn gaze for a long moment. The energy between them gave me a chill.

Then Ry clenched her lips and wound up for the pitch of a lifetime. She hurled the stone as far as she could.

The three of us stood looking at the thicket of brush where the stone had disappeared.

A red-tailed hawk screeched from the sky. Ry looked up.

Just then, another hawk appeared, and the two flew together in graceful circles above the thicket.

Ry buried her altar in the sand. We hiked out of the canyon and walked back to the group home in silence. She hugged me good-bye and went home with her mom.

Magic is nothing more than a shift in consciousness and some of the best magic seems to happen *way* outside the therapist's comfort zone. We have a duty to follow wounded children wherever they need to go to heal themselves.

You have to be willing to go to the canyon.

There Are Other Stupid Creatures

Lindsey Donner

I went back to the wrong thing often, grappling
with you on Applewood Lane

where a small sheaf of trees still blurred
red by autumn damply hid my car

dead leaves
catching loudly on the wipers.

Because I did not let anyone look
closely at me ever, no one saw you,

palming my head like a ripe fruit
pitching in the dark pool of your lap.

There are animals that go back to wrong things too,
moths on hot bulbs, seals lolling among outboard

engines, beaten dogs straggling back.

Baby Bird

Michael Hemmingson

I didn't go to that café this morning
because I remembered that
my former fiancée and her daughter
often went there
for Sunday breakfast.

How unkind to accidentally run into
the family I lost and answer
questions, the "what are you doing up
here?" kind.

The death of a fetus in Encinitas
still harasses my head, insane:
the silent eulogy for the dead
is a song I'd rather not sing again –

the five-month-old
buried in the garden of tender dirt,
my behest –

a wispy soul that's still
like a baby bird in a nest,
mouth opened wide and crying
for food, softly chewed,

by a mother who takes care
of hatchlings out of instinct,
not love.

Sleepwalking

Melissa Milazzo

In my dreams Darlene's hair is a pillar of fire. In real life it was dark brown and when she wore it in a ponytail it shone like polished wood. Dreams are nothing, a language of memory, fantasy and broken symbols. I dream every night. I wake every morning with an emptiness in me, a missing portion of myself that can be defined only by absence. Everything else in my waking life is pale, muted. My absence, my empty, it burns like fire.

I awoke to a siren the last day of the semester. Images of Darlene's hair still flickered behind my eyelids as I rolled over to look out the window. A scarlet bullet parted traffic; hooks, ladders and hoses neatly coiled. I listened to the wailing siren, imagining dancing arms of fire. Somewhere life was burning. Somewhere hot flames licked at the sky.

All of my finals were over, leaving me with no responsibilities and no agenda for the day. Habit, more than anything else, carried me to the campus coffee shop. As I walked I could tell the day would be a hot one. The morning sun was barely over the rooftops and the normally dewy campus lawn was already dry. Even the coffee shop was quiet, missing the usual pack of students desperate for caffeine. I looked out over the empty tables and found Josh. His hair made him easy to spot; it was so blond it was almost transparent. He had grown a beard since I had seen him last. With a cappuccino in one hand and a cigarette in the other he looked very European, much more sophisticated than the college boy I remembered. I sat down at his table.

"Hey Josh, how you been?"

"Alright," he smiled, flashing perfectly straight teeth.

"You're looking very Euro-trash today."

Broad shoulders shrugged beneath blue denim, but I couldn't tell whether he was pleased or embarrassed by my teasing. "Just got back from the Netherlands. I did that year abroad, you know, the study away thing."

"Really? I can't believe you've been gone a whole year." If Josh had been out of the country he wouldn't know about my sister, wouldn't ask all the questions I had been avoiding.

"Well, it's not a whole year, but it's close. I just got back a couple of days ago."

A small hope smoldered in my chest. "Get a chance to hang out with anyone yet?"

Josh shook his head. "No, it seems like everyone just finished classes and blew town."

I smiled. "Just us locals now."

Josh heaved a sigh and played at sounding disappointed. "I was going to get some Mexican food, but it's just not as good when I'm all alone."

I played along, nodding sympathetically.

"Ease my pain," Josh placed his hand over his heart then extended it to me. "Take pity on this lonely soul and accompany him to Albertos!"

I laughed and took his hand.

We took his car down to the beach and gorged on tacos. After we could eat no more Josh and I hung out in his car, listening to the radio and watching waves crash against the jetty. My feet were propped up on his dashboard. Without sandals my toes looked small and comical. I wiggled them against the windshield, glancing over to see if Josh noticed the sweaty toe prints I had left on the glass. Reclined in the driver's seat, he appeared to be asleep. His chest rose and fell slowly, as if weighed upon by the atmosphere in the car.

I leaned my seat back, finding just the right angle to be comfortable. "I like this heat," I said. "It's like something physical, like a big quilt that covers your whole body, only you don't ever take it off."

Josh rolled around in his seat to look directly at me. "I know *exactly* what you mean. When I was over in Amsterdam the summer was so weird. It wasn't cold or anything, but it wasn't hot either."

"I thought it was cold there all the time."

"Oh, I froze my nuts off in the winter," Josh laughed, "but it's just sort of a non-temperature in the summer. It felt wrong, like there was something missing."

"Tell me about it," I sighed. We lapsed into silence for a while, wearing the heat and welcoming its comfort.

"Hey," Josh nudged me. "Are you asleep?"

"No."

"Well, I got an idea."

His plans for the evening involved tequila shots and a six-pack of extremely cheap beer. I knew where this was going and I didn't mind. I was almost happy as we lay together on the avocado green carpet of his studio. We laughed as he leaned over to push down my bra strap. I rolled on to my stomach, eye level with the ground and found confetti. It was hidden in the shag, white flecked remnants of some long forgotten party. Josh rubbed his Viking whiskers across my shoulders, as if to sweep away any doubts about what we were about to do. All I could think about was the confetti. It sprouted like mushrooms from the mossy green floor of his carpet. I rolled over and put my back to it.

We turned out the lights and fucked on the living room floor. Moonlight filtered through the blinds and made zebra patterns on our bodies. I traced a line across Josh's back. He had shoulders like Atlas, huge and roped with muscle. I could feel his heat with my whole body, the throb of his heart and the air drawn in to his lungs. Below his skin, blood rushed through his veins and into his muscles, his organs, the marrow of his bones. I wrapped my arms around him, holding that sweaty body, urgent with the business of life.

That night Josh and I slept on the floor. I dreamed of Darlene again. In my dream world her hair burned more brightly than ever. We stood before the mirror in her bedroom, playing the game we had played since we were children, trying to find differences in our identically twinned bodies. She was half an inch taller than me. I had a chicken pox scar above my eyebrow. Our differences seemed minute in the face of such overwhelming sameness. Once, when we were in high school, Darlene dyed her hair. She wanted to look different, to be her own person for a while. She chose a pretty auburn color and I helped her apply it. Darlene sat on the blue plush toilet seat in my parent's bathroom while I squirted the color on her head. Blood-colored rivulets ran down her neck. We weren't careful and we stained the toilet seat. It was an accident. Darlene didn't care about the damage; she was finally different.

Three days later the light on my answering machine was still blinking with Josh's message. I gave in and called him back.

"I want to see you again," he said. "I felt like we had a real connection."

Trying to form a response was more difficult than a whole year's worth of classes. "I've been busy," was all that I could come up with.

"You still living with your folks?"

"Yeah."

"Got a job for the summer?"

"Not really." We lapsed in to an awkward silence.

"I heard about your sister. I'm so sorry, Belinda," he whispered. There was so much earnest emotion in his voice. It pained me. "When we got together that night I didn't know yet."

"That's okay," I said flatly. Everyone was sorry, so sincerely, uselessly sorry.

"Are you okay?" he asked, just as all the polite, sorry people had done before him.

"No," I answered. The line was quiet again. I had a flood of words, a sea of thoughts to drown him with, but still my mouth was dry. "I'm smaller," I began. "Sometimes I think I'm the same, but then I see I have small shoulders."

Josh answered carefully, "Well, no, you're not exactly a big person." I thought I could hear his blond whiskers brush against the phone.

"You've seen my shoulders. How am I supposed to carry on when I'm this small?"

Josh didn't have an answer. He didn't call back.

My bed was sweaty after hours of tossing around and trying to sleep. I left it and got up to visit the bathroom. I slunk down the hallway, past the plastic houseplants and neatly framed photographs, pausing when I thought I heard a noise. My toes curled deep in the carpet as I tensed, listening to see if our mother was sleeping.

Our father always snores. He snorks and growls his way through the night, announcing his slumber to the world at large, but our mother is far more subtle. She lays curled in on herself like a crescent moon, three-quarters of her mind eclipsed by undifferentiated darkness, and one-quarter still brightly aware. One-quarter of her mind stays open all night silent, distant and patient as the cold satellite that revolves around the earth. The white crescent of her body lays bright in the darkness of her bed and listens for noises in the dark. In the hallway I swayed my weight from left to right, producing an experimental squeak from the floorboards. I received nothing, save my father's snores, for an answer.

Streetlight trickled through the bathroom window, casting shadows in the basin of the sink. The countertop was cool against my skin as I laid my arm on it, inspecting the toilet seat cover. It was still blue, still plush, but it was completely free from stains. I rubbed my fingers in it, pulling apart the pile, searching for a remnant of my memory. I knelt that way for a long time, crouched on the cool bathroom tile. After a while I leaned back on my heels and tried to remember if the seat cover had been replaced since Darlene's accident, or if a stain that deep would ever fade away.

As I left the bathroom I stepped on the creaky floorboard.

"Belinda," our mother called, "What are you doing?"

I grunted noncommittally and continued down the hall.

"Go back to bed!" She yelled.

My bed, like sleep, was not an option. Moonlight leaked from the crack beneath Darlene's door. When I pushed it open I found her room cold and empty. It was neat, like she always left it, but now it reeked of antiseptic cleanliness. A big-eyed girl stared back at me from the mirror mounted on Darlene's closet door. She looked lonely without her twin.

There must be some perversion of physics that allows a body to grow larger and smaller, to vacillate within the field of size. At one time I must have been bigger. I nearly broke my shoulder that morning. I must have been more substantial to force open her bedroom door. No one else was home. No one to see how tightly she had locked herself away from the world. No one else to find her crushed into the mattress. White pills sprouted like tiny mushrooms from the surface of her vomit, which had congealed around the face. I knew I was alone when I noticed how the vomit stuck in her eyelashes, jamming them shut against the morning light.

It was twilight when I first saw Steven. He smiled at me from across a sea of faces at a party. The house belonged to someone's stepfather or uncle, all Craftsman style cabinetry and stained glass décor. The keg looked out of place in the living room, but that didn't stop anyone from using it. I was on my way to get a beer when I noticed Steven leaning against a doorjamb, drinking a beer and engrossed in conversation with a guy who looked like a junior professor. Steven sipped a beer and pushed back strands of his long dark hair, listening as the other man spoke. He bore a strong resemblance to Jesus. When he caught me staring at him, Steven brought me a plastic cup and introduced himself. He was a grad student and almost had his master's degree in literary theory.

Several cups of beer later, we migrated to the front porch. Outside the night air was refreshing after the close quarters of the party. "You have lovely eyes," he said. "You look like you know a secret."

I smiled at him. "Stig aroun an you'll find out." Our flirting was interrupted by one of his friends.

"Who's this?" the friend asked, nodding in my direction.

"This is…"

"Top Secret," I interrupted, leaving Steven hanging mid-sentence. "Who'r you?"

"I'm Dan," the friend laughed. "Man, how do you find these girls?"

I settled my ass on the porch railing and watched the two grad students strut their intellectual prowess. Words like "proleptic," "locution," and "ratiocination" sprung from their lips to float over chirping of crickets and dewy blades of grass. When Dan uttered "*mutatis mutandum*" I couldn't suppress my giggles.

"What's so funny?" Dan asked.

"Your words," I explained carefully. "Your words'r all wrong." Didn't they know they were at a party?

"We're talking about Lacan."

"La who?" I was having trouble paying attention. Everything seemed slightly fuzzy.

"Jaques Lacan - the French Freud," Dan said, obviously expecting me to be confused.

"Oh yeah, I know'm," I mumbled as dim memories flashed through my mind. "Didn't he write sumpin about Poe?"

Steven stared at me. "Wow. I'm doing my paper on Lacan and..." He started in on a detailed description of his own theory on all things literary. Meanwhile Dan wandered away.

"Language operates as a symbolic system. You see, words are signs," Steven's thin hands danced before my eyes, illustrating each of his points, gesticulating emphasis when necessary and occasionally smoothing his hair. "The sign is always a pre-supposition of the absence of the thing it denotes."

"What?"

"When we use a word, the thing we are talking about doesn't have to be there. You can say cat, talk about a cat, describe a whole world full of cats, even if there isn't one anywhere in the room. Words are not attached to physical things," he paused. "Language is empty." Silence sat between us as I considered what Steven said. "Do you understand?"

The idea surfaced slowly in my mind. "It's defined by absence."

"Not quite," he corrected.

"No!" I protested, grabbing the sleeve of his T-shirt. "I know what you mean," I could not explain how profoundly I understood the emptiness in a set of signs that had once seemed so full. I was a twin, but I had no twin. I was a sister, but I had no sibling. This was all true and it was all so wrong. Language failed me. All I could say was, "I know."

He leaned closer and put an arm around my shoulder. "Nevermind. This's a party. Let's relax." We sat quietly and sipped from our plastic cups until I had almost forgotten what he said. I leaned into the warmth of his shoulder, letting his arm engulf me like a blanket. There on the railing, melting into his body, I almost forgot about being alone.

"Hey!" My friend Stephanie leaned out the front door interrupting Steven's opportune moment. "Are you going home with us or what?" I felt him pull away from me and caught the sharp odor of his sweat.

"No," I mumbled, avoiding her eyes.

Stephanie threw the door open and stormed out on to the porch. "How you gonna get home then? You gonna fly?"

I started giggling uncontrollably, imagining myself swooping through the air while frantically flapping my arms.

"I kin fly!" I whispered to Steven, wiggling my fingers to demonstrate how I could defy gravity. "Shhhh. . . thaz my secret." The patio took a startling lurch to the left and I couldn't comprehend why.

"Look at you," Stephanie scolded, "You can't even stand up."

"But I kin fly," I corrected her.

She took my hand, her long nails pressing against my skin. "Say goodnight Miss Belinda. We're flying your ass home."

Steven and I did not exchange phone numbers. I tried to ask his learned opinion about my small shoulders, but it was rather difficult with Stephanie pulling on my arm. "Do you think I'm small?" I yelled over her shoulder as she sat me in the back seat of her car. No one answered. Steven had disappeared from the porch.

As soon as I sat down, I threw up. I managed to keep most of my soggy mess outside of the car, but some of my vomit ended up on her back seat.

"Get out, get out!" Stephanie screeched, waving her arms, as if her frantic actions could make me move faster. "Just stand there." She pointed. "Right there. We're not going anywhere until I get this cleaned up."

Fat tears burned down my cheeks, blurring my vision. I stood there, useless, as her little Toyota turned into an amorphous blob. "I'm sorry," I bawled. "It was an accident."

In my dreams I always find Darlene as I last saw her, lifeless in her bed. A strange twilight like the color of faded jeans floods through the window, providing the only illumination. It falls directly on her body, spotlighting the one grossly incongruent element in her otherwise orderly room. Her body is twisted on mattress, one arm bent awkwardly under her chin. Her face is unrecognizable. Slack and crusted with vomit, it wears none of the expressions that I have come to recognize over the nineteen years of our life. It is the face of a woman I have never seen before. Around that face, that foreign mask that is meant to represent my sister, I recognize her hair. It dances like fire, each strand a flame licking urgently at the sky.

I want to stroke her hair in my dream, to burn along with her beautiful fire, but I find myself compelled to search through her vomit. Some nights I handle swatches of carpet, broken glass, condoms, something that feels like vegetable soup. One item always remains the same: the pills. In her vomit I find a multitude of tiny white capsules strewn like confetti over her bed. I work carefully, patiently, to separate the pills from the rest of the soggy mess she disgorged. As I work my fingers through the vomit, the pills form a pile beside me. The pile is fecund. It grows, sprouting tiny new mushroom pills until I see nothing but white. Nothing is left but absence.

At night my shoulders ache and my mind burns as I search the house for Darlene. All I find is the emptiness of her room, the missing stain on the toilet seat. Eventually I go back to bed and wonder what my mother listens for in the dark.

Continuing

Larry Kuechlin

Upon water and unison,
the fire:

upon genesis
and all these silent matters:

our hands continuing;

the imperfect stars ringing
where scars are hewn;
a reflection of incite and fall
laid to rest over landscapes rising up.

Upon wing light and knowing,
the sky, waiting;
and restless night beyond;

our breath continuing;

the pathways of our bind,
touched as helpless;
uncloaked within a shadow length of

sudden words;
convergence as one darkness

becomes another.

The Storm

Dave Riessen

I was expecting the call. Any minute now the phone would ring, I'd answer and she'd be there. We'd talk about the weather, how hard the wind was blowing and how we hadn't seen it rain like this since way back when.

And then she'd say she had a pot of soup on and I was welcome to come over if I happened to be out and about in this crazy weather. Holding the phone up to her ear with her shoulder, she'd pour herself another cup of coffee and tell me she'd put on a fresh pot if I wanted to come over and play cards.

Back then, we always played cards. That was the thing with our family, we never had any money and not much food, but we always had several decks of cards. You think you can beat a twelve year old at solitaire, someone who has been playing since they were three? You're gonna get your butt kicked. Don't put any money on your winning.

And then I'd tell her the Italian Pine had grown the fullest, a beautiful tree that caused me a lot of work, having to climb through the branches once a year to thin it out.

"Can't do that with the Stone Pine," I'd say. "It's too tall. Don't know if it has enough roots to stay put on the side of the hill. I hope it doesn't fall on the house, the way this wind's blowing."

"You ought to see the wind over here, coming up the canyon. It's just crazy. I was out checking on the shed, just to make sure the doors and windows were closed. I saw some homeless people running for cover under the bridge. Sure wish they wouldn't hang out down there. It makes me nervous."

"You've got the dogs. That'll keep them away."

"The dogs don't like lightning. They were scratching at the back door and whining. I let them in and built a fire in the fireplace. You ought to see them, sprawled out all over the floor. The cats are sleeping right there with them."

"How many cats do you have now?"

"I was down to three, but then Mikki started hanging around. Now she thinks she's part of the family. She's even sleeping in between the dogs, keeping her distance from the fire, though."

"You spoil them. But then, you've always been like that."

"You kids turned out okay."

"Well, there's a lot you don't know."

"Sure is coming down. It's heading your way. About fifteen minutes, I'd guess."

"Why can't it just drizzle for a few days? Doesn't do us much good when it comes down all at once."

"Did you see the rainbow this afternoon?"

"No. Missed it."

"Looked like it was over by your house."

"Well, it didn't leave me a pot of gold."

"You sure have a nice house."

I put more wood on the fire and stirred the ashes, moving them around so that the unburned outer pieces were turned back into the middle. The fire flamed up with new life, crackling and popping enough so that I had to replace the screen.

How did I miss the rainbow? I was in and out all afternoon, collapsing the umbrellas, moving potted plants out into the rain, setting up the rain barrel. How had I missed it?

I retrieved a glass from the cupboard, filled it with ice and poured scotch over that. The bite seemed stronger than usual since I hadn't left enough room for a little water. Wincing, I went to the window and looked up at the sky toward the west, over by her house, and took another sip.

Yep. Really coming down over there. Jesus. What a storm! Probably should give her a call anyway, just to make sure she's okay. Haven't been there in a while. Maybe this weekend a game of cards would be good. A family get-together. We'll have tacos.

The phone rang. But before I could get to it they hung up. I checked the fire and returned to the window. The rain was coming down hard now, just like she'd said, about fifteen minutes.

"You're thinking about her again, aren't you?"

I didn't bother to turn around. "Yeah." I felt my eyes mist. "Every time it rains like this. And then the phone seems to ring. Have you noticed that?"

"How long's it been, three years since she passed away?"

"I guess. Seems like yesterday."

Luscious Spirit

Bridget Hanley

When a strawberry gives of its essence, all of itself,
lush and ripe against my teeth and tongue, soon to be
what keeps my body alive,
or an Heirloom tomato
melts inside me with a goodness
masked by its awkward shape and mottled skin;
my flesh becomes walking sunshine
and moonlight with toes.

And while I may collect shells on the sand
turning them over as they glitter next to the rush
of waves, every day we carry shells on our fingers.
These smooth pearlescent protective coverings
stay with us even when we sleep.

Every night
we fall into worlds we don't plan for.
Our bodies take time off
from the conscious chatter
of mind and movement of muscles.

This continual ebb and flow of here
and not here, of spirit becoming form,
of all that is
heaving and breathing as one
contains more mystery in a fingernail
than I can say.

June Gloom and Golden Sand

Erik Martin

Coronado Beach was covered in gold.

As a child, I fervently believed this. I remember walking across the hot sand from the Hotel Del Coronado to where the surf had wet the land and looking down in amazement. The brown sand was flecked with prodigious, sparkling gold dust! I ran to tell my father, who at noon was by the pool, already working on his second Johnny Walker.

"Gold? You'd better figure out how to collect it before anyone else finds out about it. Maybe you'll be able to buy that dirt bike that you've been wanting," he'd said, his words slightly slurred.

He was right, I thought. I was going to be rich. At eight years old, I already knew that being rich was like having fabulous superpowers. Forget about a dirt bike; I'd get a helicopter, or a jet pack and fly to school. The possibility seemed so vivid, so real.

So, what did I know about collecting gold? A lot, I had thought. The previous summer, my family had gone on vacation in Jamestown, California and I had learned all about panning for gold. I had even stood in a cold stream with a little pan of my own and... what? I remember playing in the water. I remember that I got cold and cried. But I must have found gold—I had a tiny vial on my shelf with a few flecks of gold dust inside of it. I was certain that once I got started it would all come back to me.

I needed a pan.

It occurred to me that my mom had bought a pie from the grocery store last night for dessert and the leftovers were in our suite's refrigerator in a tin—the perfect pan for panning gold. Our suite was right off of the beach. I raced to it, being careful to be quiet once inside. My mother was resting. She'd had a headache if I remember right—she used to get a lot of headaches. I found the pie and put the last slice onto a paper plate, which I put back into the refrigerator. I rinsed out the tin. I also took a small plastic shovel and bucket. I would need the bucket to carry my gold. I envisioned getting buckets of the shiny stuff and wondered how much each bucketful would be worth.

I think I tried to pan for about an hour before I gave up.

I remember scooping my pie tin full of wet sand and shaking it back and forth like I was supposed to. But what was left at the end didn't look like gold at all, just bigger pieces of sand and small pebbles. I could see it there lying on the ground all around me, but I could not collect the first speck. I remember picking the sand up with my hand and seeing it sparkle in my palm. But whatever it was, it was beyond my ability to isolate and gather. An elusive will-o-the-wisp of childhood.

I had been terribly disappointed. I had forgotten about that disappointment until now.

I went back and told my father. He was no longer by the pool. I found him in our suite. My mother was up then, making lunch. For some reason I remember the lunch vividly—boiled hotdogs, potato sticks, and a Twinkie.

"Dad, I couldn't get the gold," I said. "Will you help me after lunch?"

"What gold? Don't be stupid," he had said.

"But you said I have to get it before anyone else does," I whined.

"What the hell are you talking about?"

"Sweetie, come here and eat your hotdog," my mother said.

I went to the table and started to eat. Between mouthfuls, I told her about the gold.

"Sweetie, there isn't really any gold on the beach. Your father was just teasing you. It's just the sun reflecting off of minerals—probably quartz," she told me.

I was crestfallen for all of about five minutes. Then my mother asked me if I wanted to walk to the nearby store where they sold shells and shark's teeth. The mysterious gold of Coronado was forgotten, pushed out by the awesome possibility of getting shark's teeth.

It's funny that I thought of that now. I hadn't remembered the gold. It just came back as I was staring out of the window of my cab down at San Diego Bay. Such a powerful memory to have forgotten. I'm going back to the Del, back to Coronado Beach. Why would I go if there was no gold? I'm going because for years that trip that we took when I was eight seemed like the last happy time, the last normal time that my family had. And lately things haven't been going well for me. I'm hoping that by coming to the last happy place in my childhood, that maybe I'll be able to reconnect with something that I lost. It isn't a heartening sign that the first memory to come back to me, panning for gold on the beach and my tremendous disappointment at learning that there was no gold, also revealed that my father was already an erratic drunk, and my mother had already begun to have symptoms of her illness.

We passed a sign on the Coronado Bridge. It read, *Need help? Make the call. Suicide is never the answer.* There was a phone number.

Maybe this wasn't such a good idea.

When I got to the hotel and checked in, it was nearly night. The hotel looked pretty much as I remembered it. I didn't feel like going to the beach yet. Instead I walked down the street until I found a liquor store about a block away. I bought a fifth—bourbon, not scotch—I wasn't completely my father's son.

I got back to my room—a room, not a suite—I couldn't afford a suite. I poured a drink into one of the hotel glasses and turned on the television. I wasn't really watching it though. I was thinking back to our vacation and how things fell apart afterwards. It had seemed to me, as a child, that things were still good when we had vacationed here, that my parents were still in love, that we were happy. I've already realized now that this wasn't the case. My memories had been filtered through the rose-tinted—no, gold-tinted eyes of the child I had been. Memories of gold that wasn't there.

It wasn't until the vacation had ended and we had arrived back in Ohio that I had known something was wrong. My father was drunk all of the time and my parents had fought a lot. My mom was sick—headaches she said. A year later, they separated and then divorced. I lived with mom at first. I was ten. But her behavior became as bizarre and erratic as my father's, even though she never drank. When I was eleven, we learned that she had a brain tumor. When I was twelve, she died.

I drank more than half of the fifth of bourbon on my first night back at the Hotel Del. At some point I passed out.

When I awakened, my head was pounding and I was terribly thirsty. Surprisingly, I had undressed sometime before passing out. Rather than face my hangover, I used my standard cure. I took three Advil and washed them down with a large glass of cold water. Then I went back to bed for two more hours.

At ten-thirty I got up again feeling much better. I opened the curtain and saw a gray sky hanging over the San Diego coast. I thought it was always sunny in Southern California, but I guess overcast skies are common at this time of year. 'June gloom' I had heard someone call it. Just as well, I wasn't feeling very sunny myself.

I thought about the bridge and the sign. *Need help? Make the call. Suicide is never the answer.*

I ate an overpriced breakfast in a restaurant near the hotel along with three, eight-dollar mimosas. Then I walked down to Coronado Beach.

It was gray and actually chilly by the water. The beach was still full of people on vacation from places like Cleveland, Philadelphia, and Chicago, who, maybe like me, had never heard of 'June gloom' and were trying to pretend that it didn't exist and that they were in a tropical paradise. I had to admit, it was pretty even with the haze. Point Loma was a silhouette off to the right and some island sat off to the left. I'd have to ask someone what that was. The palm trees in San Diego were majestic, unlike the stunted little things I remember seeing on the east coast in Myrtle Beach.

I took off my shoes. The sand was cool and clean. I walked down the beach not going close to the water yet. I was almost afraid to go to that place where the surf came onto land. Afraid that I would see something there that I wouldn't like.

But eventually I did walk down to the water. I'm not sure what I had been afraid of, but whatever it was, it wasn't there. It was just water—cold, foamy water. It was surprisingly cold. I didn't remember that from the last trip. The Atlantic is like a primordial bath, eighty-five degrees this time of year. The Pacific here had to be twenty degrees colder than that, but for some reason, maybe because it was colder, it seemed cleaner.

I didn't see any gold.

I walked back to the hotel. My heart felt as heavy as the Pacific was cold.

I went to the hotel bar and ordered a bourbon. I only had one, not because I was trying to stay sober, but because I wanted to get drunk. At hotel prices I was going to run out of cash well before total inebriation. So I left the Del again. I was hungry and saw a self-proclaimed Irish pub with a large patio. I found a small empty table. I ordered the fish and chips and a Johnny Walker—it seemed appropriate just then.

A couple near me had a dog. I was surprised this was allowed in a restaurant, even on the patio. People were eating, I mean. But no one paid any attention to it. Even when the dog took a piss on a chair leg and I watched the urine run into a drain, no one seemed to care—California.

The fish and chips were way too greasy, even for me who had been a regular at Steve's Hotdogs in Cleveland for years. Another California stereotype demolished—everything wasn't just about being healthy. To top it off, someone lit a cigarette on the other side of the dog people. The dog people gave him a dirty look and said something to one another, but apparently smoking was allowed as the waitress brought him an ashtray. I pulled out my own pack of Marlboro Lights and lit up. Now the dog people had something to be really upset about. A minute later, they got up and left, taking their ill-mannered, pissing dog with them.

At some point I found my way inside. You couldn't smoke in there, but it was darker and dingier and I felt more at home. I had come to San Diego to try to recapture something, but so far I felt just like I had at home. It was cloudy, chilly, dirty, and I was drunk. It was as if I had never left Cleveland.

Eventually, I reached that rarified level of intoxication where I was able to clearly see those years after my mother died and I had gone to live with my father. Early on, we still had money and even though he drank too much and was occasionally violent, it wasn't too bad. It wasn't until Cleveland's economy fell apart in 2000 or so and he lost the business and then the house that it got really bad. I was sixteen then. We had to move into a little shithole apartment on Lorain Avenue. I got a job at USA Gas and he—well, he drank. I am not going to go into the fights or the times I would come home and find him unconscious on the couch with his pants full of crap. Needless to say, it wasn't a happy home. I told him that I hated him more than once.

I left the day I turned eighteen.

Two years later, he called me and told me that the doctor told him that he had cirrhosis. I don't remember what I said, but I wasn't very nice. I had only spoken to my dad twice since I had left.

A year later, shortly after I turned twenty-one, I saw him in a bar. He looked yellow and was a lot thinner than I remembered. He had a scotch in his hand—not Johnny Walker; he couldn't afford it by then—this was the really cheap stuff, gutter scotch. We talked a little, not about his drinking or his disease, but about me and about mom. He asked what I was doing, if I was dating anyone. He told me a story about mom—apparently she had started doing some odd things before they had separated. One night, he said I had stayed over at friend's house who was having a birthday sleepover, so he and mom had decided to have a romantic evening. He bought a bottle of wine and some cheese and bought mom roses. He had some rose petals, too. He spread them on the bed and on the floor of their bedroom. Everything went great right up to the point they went into the bedroom. He told me that mom had seen the petals and it was like someone had flipped a switch in her head.

"Look at this mess," he said doing a passable imitation of mom. "It is an absolute, disgraceful mess in here."

At which point, Dad said, the romantic evening was over as mom got it into her head to vacuum and clean the whole house from top to bottom.

"It was eleven at night," he told me. "That was the first really odd thing I noticed. Then there were the headaches. I never once even considered though that she might be sick. I was too wrapped up in my own sickness. I thought she did that kind of stuff to get back at me for drinking. I've always wondered if I had done something differently, maybe things would have turned out better."

He stared into the mirror behind the bar, but I got the impression that he was looking at something else entirely. I didn't say anything. I didn't know what to say. I didn't have the experience, the empathy, the words—nothing. Today, I understand a little more clearly what he was feeling.

After a brief second where I thought he was going to cry, he was back to being his gruff, surly self. He asked me to spot him some money for a few more drinks. I gave him a twenty. He said that maybe we would get together for Christmas. I said, sure, maybe.

He died on the twenty-third of December.

Need help? Make the call. A fall two hundred feet into cold darkness. I had heard somewhere that killer whales used to be common in San Diego Bay a hundred years ago. Wouldn't that have been a sight? I wondered what was in the bay tonight? I thought that I would finish my drink and then find out.

"Hey sweetie, can I have one of those cigarettes?" said a gravelly voice.

I looked at the wreck of a woman on the stool next to me and realized she was talking to me.

"What? Yeah sure," I said, handing her one.

"You want to come smoke with me?" she asked. "Come on. Bring your drink."

I followed her. Why not?

Outside, she introduced herself.

"My name's Audrey," she said. She looked like she might have been pretty once, but the sun and alcohol had aged her prematurely. I bet she was no older than thirty-five, but she looked fifty. Her smile was warm though and something in her tone was reassuring.

"Tom," I said.

We talked and smoked and I bought us more drinks. At some point we staggered back to my room.

"This is really nice," she said. "I've lived around here all of my life but I've never stayed here."

"It's okay. I stayed here when I was a kid. I wanted to come back for some reason."

Audrey spent the night in my room, but we didn't sleep together—sex, I mean. We just talked. I know it sounds cliché, but that was all. For an evening, I allowed her to direct where my mind went. It's probably not a way to live your life, but I didn't think anymore that night about suicide hotline signs and marine monsters lurking in the bay.

The next day, I was much less hung over than I had a right to be. Not so with Audrey. She looked worse than she had the night before, but she took a shower and that helped a little. She kept saying that she had to go, but it was sunny and I pleaded with her to walk down to the beach with me before she left. I had no desire to take over responsibility for myself again. I bought her some coffee and she finally relented.

Once she decided to walk with me, she wasn't anxious anymore. We got down to where the waves were rolling in, wetting the sand. There, spread out like a nebula, were the glittering gold flecks that had dazzled me as a child.

"It's beautiful," I said. "You know, when I was a kid I saw this beach and was convinced that all of those sparkles were gold. I was crushed when my mom told me they weren't."

"No—they probably are," she said. "Gold dust gets washed in with the sand on a lot of California beaches. I went to Gold Bluffs Beach once up north and read this whole thing on how the prospectors would pan an ounce or two a day from some of the beaches. Yeah, that probably is gold. Not really worth anything, not enough and too hard to get."

It was worth a great to me. I don't know if what she told me was true. I've never looked it up. I've never wanted to. Right then I accepted her words as if they had been handed down from God Himself. I stared down at the sand, at the tiny, shining specks that had briefly meant everything to a child.

Tears welled up in my eyes. I tried to push them down and it made them push back harder until I just let go and cried uncontrollably—for the first time that I could remember.

"Hey, what wrong? Are you all right?" Audrey asked.

She could have walked away, or been freaked out by my sudden fountain of tears. Instead, she held me, right there on the beach with the waves lapping our feet. That scarecrow of a woman who was a veritable stranger, except for what we had shared last night, had unwittingly brought this on with her words and now she helped me through it.

"It okay, Tom, you're all right," she said.

And I really was. I won't claim to have had a life-changing epiphany. I struggled after that for a long time. I still do. But that was the moment I was able to let go a lot of the past, including my guilt and my many regrets, and take back the one thing that I had been missing for a long time.

Coronado Beach really is covered in gold—and I felt hope again.

Almost Gone

Janice Coy

She sits behind a porous curtain of green and blue bamboo strands that hang from the ceiling near her desk. Her bedroom is dim; a flickering candle disperses the scent of ripe peaches.

The glow of her computer screen is on her high cheekbones and straight nose. Her cell phone pulses and she responds, fingers tapping the buttons. White wires emerge from beneath her salon-layered hair, caress her jawbone, rest against her breasts. I hover in the doorway.

Unnoticed.

When she leaves the next morning, I reach out, pull the too low zipper on the front of her dress higher and kiss her cheek. Her hair smells of warm raspberries. She laughs.

She pretends not to like our routine. But I know she does. I can tell from the way she half-heartedly dodges my lips, acts like she's going to outrun me. Like she could in those boots.

She juggles a travel mug in one hand, a wad of keys in the other. The large black purse on her shoulder bulges with notebooks. She cradles an Economics book in one elbow. The sun is still low over the neighbor's roof, when she backs out of the driveway in her lipstick red car, and disappears around the corner.

I trust she's headed to high school.

I linger in the drive.

Mothers, fathers hurry by holding their children's hands. Some have pink backpacks slung over their shoulders. Others adjust sweaters, zip jackets. I can hear the elementary school bell across the street, it's urgent trill. The parents quicken their pace; their children jog beside them. I want to tell them to slow down. To enjoy the weight of their child's hand in theirs.

I learned to savor the moments with my daughter – she's my third. But moments fade. Seasons progress. I can see the passing of time in the quiet, neat rooms of my too-big house and I yearn for the days of scattered toys and sticky chins.

It's the night of winter formal. I stand with unfamiliar parents in a strange living room. A cold drink wets the palm of my hand. I munch on a dry cracker spread with smoked cheese. My daughter's midnight blue cocktail dress floats above her knees. Her crystal earrings spark and swing with the tilt of her head. She chats with her friends, face animated. A limo waits out front to whisk them to the dance when we are done with our photographs.

She turns and beckons me over. She wraps her arm around my shoulders. Bends to kiss my cheek. The photographer's camera flashes.

"Love ya mom."

And then she's gone, trailing the fragrance of Strawberries in Champagne.

Bikini Days

Sharon Rosen Leib

My three teenage daughters wear
scalene triangles of fabric
leaving plains of unblemished,
virgin skin on display
for the world to see, admire, desire.

My own bikini days expired eighteen years –
a short lifetime – ago,
sacrificed on the altar of child bearing and
suburban motherhood.

Now a Speedo one piece carries me through
the waters revealing
skin mottled by pinpoint freckles and
thumbnail age spots and
the lower meridian of my tush.

But this doesn't stop me from swimming
forty laps - stroking and kicking through
the high tides and low ebbs.

Just Do It

Judy Geraci

When he walked in the door and saw all those umpires waiting for him to make a decision, Joe went for the familiar. None of those cross-trainers, air-pump, spring-loaded, fancy things. He wanted plain old tennis shoes. He hadn't played tennis since high school, over ten years ago. Ten. Tennis. It all fit. If he said it over and over, it sounded like tennashoes, the way a little kid might say. Tenna could also be an abbreviation for antenna. He certainly picked up signals from these shoes. They were sending him all kinds of messages.

While the police transported him to the station, Joe heard their voices honking like deep-throated geese: "AWOL, AWOL." He tried to understand the message, what it meant. His brain shuffled memories like a deck of slippery cards. The King of Spades pointed him back to his big mistake, the one that landed him in a squad car. At the time, it seemed like a great idea to jump the net with his new tennis shoes. He still didn't understand how he landed in the McPlayland ball pit with a dozen screeching toddlers and their mothers tugging at his arms and legs.

The cops took him to the county hospital, where they shot him full of drugs. After he woke up, two guys in greens bolstered him at the elbows like shelf brackets and led him into a taxi that looked like an ambulance. Joe scanned his limbs, chest and abdomen with his hands for injuries. When his fingers read the pimpled Braille on his forehead, he understood that his brain had fallen out and he was going to the ER to get a replacement. Instead, they returned him to Tri-City's South Unit, the place from which he'd strayed.

Locked in safety, Joe settled back into the routine: three meals a day, meds, and clean clothes, with sleeping in between. At first they let him sleep and sleep, dreaming in and out, one day into the next. But after a while, they made him get up, threatening to reduce his meds if he couldn't. The aides forced him to shower and handed him some nubby grey tube socks and a baggy sweat suit from the clean clothes bin. Once on his feet, Joe automatically fixed his eyes on the top of his new sneakers to steady himself. He stared at the white leather, simple, free of cluttering adornments, and felt a peace he hadn't known in years.

"AWOL, AWOL," suddenly became clear. A wall was exactly what he needed. Joe scuffed his way down the waxed hallway. His eyes scanned the walls foot by foot, until he found the just-right sweep of plaster. He pressed his back against it and waited until he felt firmly bonded, like quick-set cement, then scootched his heels out a couple of inches from the metal baseboard so he could view his new shoes in their entirety.

Joe was weary; bone-tired of making mistakes. His girlfriend had been a mistake, his kid, his haircut, all of it. As he stared down at his shoes, Joe decided they were the only good decision he'd ever made. And in that moment, he realized that if he didn't move any more than absolutely necessary, he could avoid ever screwing up again. He slid his eyes along the shoestrings and threaded himself down the rabbit hole of the first eyelet. He ratcheted himself hand-under-hand, a climber descending Half-Dome. The white laces, strong and sturdy, capped with smooth plastic tubing, held him neatly.

"Does he ever move?"

Joe heard the whisper and pulled to the surface. A group of new hires—aides and custodians—gathered in the hall for their orientation. Of course he moved. Couldn't they see he was standing up, dressed? Did they think someone carried him like a cardboard cut-out and propped him here? Just because he didn't talk, didn't mean he was deaf or dumb. Joe pushed off the wall and shuffled to another spot to be left alone. He adjusted his stance and once again slid down the braided cord of memory to the place where time twisted the years and hours.

Joe wheeled around his earliest years in a big-bumpered walker with a wrap-around tray, where bits of bland, pre-chewed food occasionally appeared. He rarely played with the squeaky balls and spinners that dangled within his reach, but instead delighted in bumping into the tall legs that towered above him, buckling their knees. Sense memories flickered on the gauze screen of his mind, blurring one into another—swathed and swaddled in cotton, smeared with unguents and ointments, oily odors drifting in and out. He felt the swoosh of air on his ears, his baby body tossed up and down, and then flying like a football. His dad laughing while his mom made funny sounds. The whizzing air, the things that flew around him—skillets and steak knives.

The shoe started cinching up around the top. Joe sometimes got that feeling, visiting his childhood too long. He scaled the laces, arm-over-arm, then dropped back down through the second set of eyelets, where it was a little roomier, and settled down on the deck of swabbie life, the gentle rocking where he'd built his skills and confidence as a young man in refrigeration repair. That nice recruiter with the eagle eyebrows sat across from Joe and encouraged him even though he scored low on the AFSQT abilities index.

"I always tested bad in school," Joe explained. "Mom always said it was probably on account of the wine she drank to keep down the nausea during pregnancy. I'm on the slow side, but I can learn, if you give me time."

"No problem," the recruiter answered. "You tested at Class IV, and that's definitely trainable. Matter of fact, we're taking in a lot Class IVs this year on account of the shortages. Class V's the bottom 10%, and they're strictly prohibited. But you're up here at 13%, well above the cut-off."

Unfortunately, when his separation time came from the Navy, nobody had cooling systems remotely similar to the ones Joe recognized, and he couldn't figure out how the dang things worked. How could this have happened when his sergeant had assigned him to a job he said "matched his skills and intelligence perfectly?"

Once again, the shoe began feeling a trifle clammy. Joe resurfaced, coming up for air. He hauled himself out on the smooth, dry leather to rest, like a swimmer splashing onto the warm concrete edge of the pool. He heard a voice. Was it the lifeguard calling through a bullhorn? He listened until he recognized the microphoned voice coming through the overhead speakers.

"Good Afternoon, South Unit residents. This is Dorothy with today's lunch menu. For those on regular diet, we have teriyaki grillers on your choice of white or fried rice, Oriental vegetable mix, and for dessert . . . crustless cherry cobbler. All South Unit residents please present to the dining hall for lunch."

Joe shuffled toward the large open room, ducked under the swag of plastic ivy that hung from the door frame, and inhaled the familiar steam of green beans, Bisquick and canned fruit. Joe didn't mind the food as much as some people did. The dry bread cut through the fuzzy tongue his meds caused, and every so often certain smells cleared his foggy mind. Like a sudden change in weather, electrochemical conditions lined up and Joe switched on to "the real world." And after a few minutes of watching people talk to their mashed potatoes and hearing the King Tut man shouting obscenities, Joe's brain flicked itself back to the comfort of cushioned leather.

He made his way toward the far end of a long row of rectangular tables to his usual spot, next to the bussing carts. He counted the glass vases with plastic flowers until he got to the fourth from the end. Joe found the particular arrangement of paintings that hung on the facing wall the most conducive to mind travel. His favorite featured a snow-swept mountain range with a single moose on a high drift, encircled by sky-high pines. His only real complaint was the way the tablecloth sometimes blocked his view to the floor, where his shoes waited patiently for their next excursion.

After a while though, Joe noticed that he lost big chunks of time inside his shoes—especially on nights and weekends, when fewer staff were around to interrupt his journeys. Even worse, he was getting lost within the shoes themselves and finding it harder to work his way out. The laces were extraordinary in their tensile strength and ability to dangle him over ravines he thought he'd already escaped and never wanted to revisit. He didn't want to see himself at the airport with that terrible haircut, shaking a tambourine, or watch himself wrestled into a restraint jacket. And he especially didn't want to see the newborn in the isolette with its wrinkled raisin skin around those toothpick bones.

"CINDY!" Joe bellowed an animal death sound. "THE BABY!"

"All right, people, leave the man alone. Sideshow's over." The familiar voice of LaVonne, South Unit's favorite aide, rang through the hall.

"I don't blame you, man," she said, shooing the others along. "Those Hairy Christmas like to drive anyone insane; you know what I'm saying? You're just gullible, is all. No crime in that."

LaVonne's voice lit Joe's brain like the strike of a match against the dull black stripe on the box. One sharp word and—sfwtzz! The scent of sulfur snapped him back.

"Matter of fact," she continued, "you're one of the better ones here. Do wish you'd wipe that spittle out the corners of your mouth for yourself once in a while, though."

Joe raised the back of his hand to his dried lips and rubbed a chalky streak onto his wrist bone.

"See there, I knew someone's in there. Who can fault a man for trippin' around his own mind in this place? I sure would if I was stuck here 24/7. Eight hour shift and I'm 'bout to go Looney Tunes myself."

The truth. Joe still recognized it when he heard it. Why would anyone want to come back to life here? He didn't. He wanted his tennashoes to take him back to somewhere nice, where he could be at peace, like they did in the beginning. But now they took him further, into the darkest place of all.

He'd married way too young, straight out of high school. Cindy had a cute face and nice titties, laughed at his jokes, and made him feel smart. She worked nights in a local deli, a classy place with thick sandwiches and decent coleslaw. Joe could hear the muffled crunch of cabbage and carrot shreds between his teeth, smell the mayonnaise and vinegar in his mind's nostrils. He remembered how he liked to drop in sometimes and watch her from the counter. The way she constantly tucked her hair behind her ear, her funny little sniff, her twitchy smile, all endeared her to him. How could he have known, not being a drug user himself? Not until they took the baby away at the hospital, did he hear about any of it.

The OB nurse had set her man-sized hand on his shoulder. "Sir, could you follow me please? We need to talk."

Joe's stomach and heart flash-fused into one fierce barb. "Something's wrong with the baby?" he'd asked, knees shaking. Beneath him, the floor turned to quicksand.

"Sit here, sir. Put your head between your knees, that's it. Slow breaths"

"Making that baby is the best thing I've ever done." Joe heard his voice crack and wobble, "The only thing that I started that got finished. Please. Say my baby is alive."

"Yes sir, the baby's alive." "Cindy? Oh my God, Cindy!"

"Your girlfriend is fine, but she's not too happy right now. She's very upset and angry."

"The baby's fine and Cindy's upset? I don't understand. Why can't I see them?"

The nurse rolled up a stool next to him.

"Sir, I need you to look at me and pay attention."

He felt her two hands press down on his knees, as if to keep him from floating off.

"Your girlfriend drank alcohol and used methamphetamine this morning. Your baby is going through withdrawal and, believe me, you don't want to see that."

"What? Cindy had a glass of wine to relax the pains, but I swear that's it. She doesn't do drugs, I swear. She'd never do anything to hurt our baby. It's gotta be a mistake."

The nurse stood up and shook her head with a sad smile. "Of course. Case of mistaken identity. Happens all the time. The mom always denies it. We did a tox screen and it came out positive. We can re-do it as many times as you like, but it's still going to come out positive. The proof is in, and I'm sorry sir, but mom is going to detox and the baby is going into protective custody."

"But I can take care of her. I already bought the Pampers and everything. I promise, I'll do whatever you tell me, but please don't take the baby."

"I'm sorry, sir. It's the law. We can't do anything else about it. If you'd like, you can request a paternity test and take it to court."

Joe steadied himself against the wall. He felt himself turning to wood from the feet up and the head down. And then he heard the snap of his heart—a crack of lightning, the tree trunk split all the way through. Falling like felled timber, hitting his head, and landing his first hospitalization.

When the hospital set him free— no longer a danger to himself or others—he wandered confused and hungry until he found a line of free food. The cooks took him in, bathed him in honey water, oiled and patchoulied him, swathed and swaddled him in white cotton. He felt clean and holy. This was peace, even if it came with bad hair and a turban. Until the meds ran out and they left him at the airport with a basket of change. He never saw Cindy or the baby again.

Desperately, Joe fanned his toes trying to shift to the scene, hoping somehow to land in a peaceful snowscape. Instead, he traveled to hellish territory, visions of places he'd never gone before: his silhouette on the floor surrounded by empty vials, his own body drained of blood, wrists slit; his broken neck in a noose, shoes dangling in mid-air.

"Aht's and Crahfts, South Unit, Aht's and Crahfts, please meet in the Rec Room in five minutes." The lilting voice of the art therapist warbled over the loud speaker, bringing Joe back from his hall of horrors. He followed the crowd dragging themselves to class as they were required to do every Tuesday afternoon. He entered the recreation room squeezing through the gap between the accordion-pleated doors that separated the chaos of creativity from the order of the dining hall. Joe dropped himself in his usual paint-speckled chair in the third left hand row. Slowly, the four long rows of folding chairs creaked in succession, as the residents of South Unit filtered in. From the sounds of the plastic sheeting on the tables crinkling and the rubber feet of the chairs scooting, Joe guessed that the room was filled, but didn't lift his eyes to count his classmates. Instead, he locked his vision on his tennashoes, and listened as the tiny bird of a therapist proceeded to demonstrate the craft of the day while preaching her weekly mission of self-help through creative expression.

"Today is your chance to make a fetish," she spoke slowly and clearly with purpose. "And I don't mean an obsession like a foot fetish." She paused to shush a snicker, as Joe felt all eyes light on his head. "This fetish is a type of symbolic sculpture. If something has been particularly bothering you, you can bring it outside of yourself and put it here on the table where you can address it." She thumped her tiny palm down on the table with amazing force for a woman so small that she had to perch on a stool to be seen.

"We will be working with Sculpey, a highly durable and elastic material that you can shape any way you like, but will dry hard. Put your hearts and souls into your work, ladies and gentlemen, because when you finish, you may find yourself transformed. That thing that was most bothering you will be yours to shape and control however you want."

Joe jerked his head up. Put your soles into it? When he looked up, her bright round eyes sparkled at him over the purple rims of her reading glasses, and she flashed a smile that seemed to project a mischievous knowing. He felt his shoes faintly buzzing with tension at the change he envisioned. For the first time in as long as he could remember, Joe actually felt like doing something. Something different than tennashoe travel. Something more than foreseeing his death. He was ready to create, to Make Something. He was going to take a stand with his shoes, give them a chance to redeem themselves, to turn them away from their evil expeditions.

He reached across the table and wrapped his hands around two sticks of white Sculpey, laid them in front of him, and began molding and re-molding the story of his life. He twisted and pressed and poked every detail into place, capturing every snag and ripple from the beginning, moment by moment, lesson by lesson, the way he'd been forced to re-live them these last few months. He repaired as he recreated: the DNA unwrapped, sperm and egg separated.

He reproduced his shoes with the most exacting elaborate details with one exception—he filled the shoes solid. Left no opening in which to descend. For the final touch, he rolled two skinny snakes, wrestled them into submission, and plastered them crisscrossing over the tongue's surface, tying up the loose ends.

At times of intense concentration, Joe's sense of hearing grew especially acute. He heard the soft roll of rubber wheels as the pleated doors slid open. He listened to crepe-soled footsteps of the orientation tour filling the space in the row behind him. He could hear their necks craning, the in and out of their breathing, and then the low voice of the tour guide. Joe hovered protectively around his work, and rounded his back in an unsuccessful attempt to shield his creation from view.

"Now this is really something," a deep voice whispered. "The guy at the end has been practically catatonic for weeks. But, today—look!"

Joe's toes did a little wiggle of pride.

"The details are so realistic," another voice added. "I wonder what it means—Like walk a mile in my shoes?"

Joe's toes lifted and hung in the space between tongue and insole, holding their breath.

"More like running away," the first voice returned, "This guy's gone AWOL how many times? For someone who never moves, he sure disappears easily. The truth is he spends hours leaning against the wall, looking at his feet. Might've been encouraging if he'd revealed some deeper thinking. But an aerial view of tennis shoes? I think that's pretty representative of what's going on in there."

Joe's toes collapsed, as the crepe-soled voices moved on with a muffling of hmmms, and ohhhhs. The shoes now loomed in front of him like two white headstones, and the laces were spelling his epigraph. Joe stood up, walked to the front, and got his activity card stamped. Leaving his sculpture behind, he walked down the hall and back to his room. He shut the door behind him, against daytime rules, and sat down on the edge of his bed. Slowly and carefully, he pulled the long laces all the way out and tossed the shoes in the wastebasket, the tongues panting with exhaustion. We did our best, they seemed to say. Can't you give us one more chance? They looked so pitiful. Maybe if he could just snap the laces in half ...he'd go back to the rec room, stomp that therapist with those stupid Sculpey feet, and take off once and for all. Joe wrapped the shoelaces around his two hands, stuck his sorry foot against the string and pushed to no avail. Unable to break the strings, he stared up at the ceiling, the curtain hooks that parted the room, and pondered the forces that turned nylon into Kryptonite. Then he tied the laces together and looped them into a large, sturdy slipknot, with the peace of knowing that even if this were his biggest mistake ever, it would be his last.

Rigid

Seretta Martin

There is at least one on every block.
This angry boy shuts
his bedroom door to keep out
another argument in the hall,

fingers his action figure
Stretch Armstrong doll,
pliable plastic, freakish and real—
the replica of a strong man.

He tweaks bulgy muscles, twists
the head backwards, stretches
viscous legs like rubber bands,
ties its arms around his boyish neck.

Ignoring a warning
to store the doll
sheltered from air,
he wants to feel tough, opens

the second-story window,
hurls his doll into space.
It bounces off the porch roof,
and lands with a thud in early weeds.

His mother, stunned
to find it twisted stiff, wants to know
what her son was thinking, when
he chose to destroy his favorite doll.

BEWARE LYING ALIEN FREAKS!

Scott Barbour

WHO I AM AND WHO I'M NOT – September 8

I started this blog to correct some misconceptions about me. For starters, I am not, as Conner Richardson and other members of the soccer team claim, a "freshly mainstreamed retard spaz"—or "spaztard," for short. Also, I was not kicked out of a series of schools for picking fights, starting fires or making terrorist threats against students, teachers and janitors. Nor have I ever served time in juvenile hall, a mental hospital or a group home for severely emotionally disturbed teens.

No, I am simply Jimmy Carton, grade 7, a transfer student from another school—a far superior school with a curriculum specializing in higher-order reasoning, top-secret weapons development, Israeli espionage techniques, martial arts, anti-liberal propaganda tactics, and KICKASS GAMING SKILLS. I would love to tell you the name of the school, but I am under strict orders from the DOD, CIA and NWA to maintain operational secrecy.

Now that I have introduced myself and put to rest a few honest misconceptions about me, I look forward to a fruitful year of stimulating academic pursuits with my new peers at Lyndon Baines Johnson Middle School. Let's learn!

MY SUPPOSED FITS – September 14

Some of you must not have read my previous blog entry, because the rumors about me continue. The latest ones involve my supposed fits. One story goes that I fell on the floor in the middle of Ms. Herman's social studies class and kicked the chair legs while drooling and staring blankly. Another story goes that I dropped my tray in the cafeteria, fell face-first into my tater tots and cherry jello cubes, and peed my pants.

Lies.

First, I don't even like cherry jello cubes.

Second, I've never had a fit in my life.

It's true that I sometimes practice my martial arts skills at unusual times, such as in social studies or while carrying my cafeteria food tray. But when you get to my level of martial arts proficiency, it's important to practice when people least expect it. This is an ancient strategy for keeping your chi in balance while confusing and intimidating your enemies.

So what looked like an epileptic fit to the untrained eye in social studies was really a secret technique passed down from the Ming Dynasty—a combination of karate, tai chi, jujitsu, and Kung Pao. What looked like a blank stare was intense introspection and a gathering of my chi energy to a point of maximum concentration and power. What looked like weak, contorted limbs were really lethal weapons primed for attack.

Also, any liquid that may have seeped from my bladder in the cafeteria was not urine but rather a poisonous fluid produced by the force of my will and the strength of my mind. If you had dared touch it, it would've shut down your central nervous system, leaving you a diaper-wearing vegetable for the rest of your pathetic life.

MY SO-CALLED IMAGINARY MONKEY – September 16

The rumors continue. The latest one is that I'm crazy because I talk to myself in algebra and at lunch in the cafeteria. Some people even say that yesterday I was crying and rocking and saying, "Charles, bring the pain," over and over while Conner Richardson and his buddies stood around and called me names.

More lies.

First, I have never cried once in my life. Not even when chopping onions or walking on hot coals while juggling chain saws.

Second, I was not talking to myself. I was talking to Charles.

A lot of people say Charles is not real. For example, my dad says I made Charles up to blame for all the crazy things I supposedly do. My psychiatrist, Dr. Sidney Frankenburger (aka, Sigmund Frankenstein), says Charles is a "protection" of my "altered ego." The way he explains it, there are parts of me that I think are bad, so I pretend they're not part of me but are instead part of a monkey named Charles. The problem with this theory is that I happen to know for a fact that Charles is not bad. In fact, he is the MOST RIGHTOUS creature in existence and my most loyal friend.

To prove the realness of Charles, I will ask you one question: can an imaginary monkey whisper in your ear that you are descended from Xerxes the Great and that you are destined to rule the world? No, only a real monkey can do that. Thus, Charles is real.

If you still are not convinced that Charles is a genuine monkey, I invite you to join me AND Charles behind the racquetball courts after school for a demonstration of Charles's REAL monkey skills— specifically, snapping off fingers, scooping out eyeballs, and peeling ears off the sides of heads. Hope to see you there!

THEY LIVE AMONG US AND THEY WANT TO EAT YOUR PANCREAS – September 21

I now have proof that Mr. Gonzales, my history teacher, is an alien and is part of the conspiracy to enslave the human race and eat our organs. My evidence is the "F" he gave me on my Civil War history paper, in which I supplied irrefutable evidence of alien landings in Roswell, New Mexico, in 1947 and the Dallas-Fort Worth metro area in 1972. I then explained that at least 69 percent of the human race has been replaced by aliens pretending to be humans, including 62 percent of the soccer team, 33 percent of the yearbook staff, Vice Principal Dr. Chudasama, and my dad.

According to Gonzales, my paper, in addition to lacking credible sources, had nothing to do with the Civil War. Oh, really? How else would you describe a war between humans and aliens for the future of America? If that's not a Civil War, then what is?

Here is the conclusion of my report, on which I am sure you will agree I deserved an A+:

On the day of the great alien uprising, the visitors will show no mercy. Razor-sharp claws will spring from the fingertips of all aliens disguised as humans, including most of our parents, teachers and fellow students. The visitors will then tear open all humans and extract their hearts, spleens, livers, kidneys and other blood-engorged morsels. After feasting on our organs, the aliens will use our intestines as dental floss and our heads as balls for a leisurely game of lawn bowling.

During the uprising, I will be safe in the backyard within my perpetual ring of fire. If any aliens breach my defenses, I will fight them off with one of the 11 martial arts in which I am an official registered black belt. For evidence of my martial arts skills, go to You Tube and view the video entitled *XtremePainMasterX*. The video shows me in the backyard looking TOTALLY FREAKING AWESOME practicing my nunchucks with no shirt on. (Note: The nunchucks may appear to be two paper towel tubes strung together with yarn, but in truth they were hand-crafted by Chinese nunchuck master Chun King especially for human-alien combat.)

IS THE FIRST AMENDMENT TOILER PAPER? – September 23

Do you think it's a coincidence that the Founding Fathers put freedom of speech in the First Amendment? That's even before guns. You wouldn't know it the way Vice Principal/Alien Invader Chud keeps trying to silence my incisive commentary and TOTALLY TRUE account of the ongoing alien invasion and impending organ-eating orgy.

Chud says it's a violation of school policy to tell the truth about scientifically verifiable phenomena, such as the fact that his blood is yellow and his pee is purple. Also that he lives in a dumpster behind Peking Palace Restaurant on Montgomery Street, where he receives coded messages from the home planet on discarded fortune-cookie fortunes.

According to Chud, my generous offer of a monkey-skills demonstration was a threat and therefore a violation of the school's zero tolerance violence policy. He also claims that my blog telling the truth about the alien invasion is "inappropriate" due to "implied threats of violence" and "derogatory characterizations of members of the faculty and student body."

First, since when did an invitation to a wildlife demonstration become a threat of violence?

Second, since when did telling the truth become "inappropriate" in America? I mean, is this why Thomas Jefferson crossed the Delaware and fought at Waterloo? Is this why Benjamin Franklin wrote the Declaration of Independence and invented lightning?

CARTON FOR PREZ – September 27

In response to VP Chud's attempts to strip us all of our rights and freedoms, not to mention our gallbladders and spleens, I hereby declare my candidacy for student body president of Lyndon Baines Johnson Middle School! My fellow students, vote for me, Jimmy Kickass Carton, if you love America and all your body parts. I promise an end to the dress code, unlimited Internet porn in the library, and snack and soda machines in every classroom.

Once in power, I will expose the fraud known as Vice Principal Chud for the evil, scaly, yellow-blooded monster he truly is. Then I will save the student body—at least those of you who are still human—from enslavement and painful organ extraction at the hands of the fiends posing as gym coaches and algebra teachers.

As a safety precaution, following the eradication of the aliens, a transitional period of iron-fisted totalitarianism will be required to prevent re-infestation by the extraterrestrial scourge. The current student body bylaws will be replaced with a constitution written by me. Next, a portrait of me posing in front of a fighter jet in aviator shades and a bomber jacket will be hung in every classroom. Following the pledge of allegiance each morning, all students and teachers will bow to my portrait and shout, "Jimmy rocks!" Also, all female members of the cheering squad will blow a kiss to the portrait upon entering and exiting any classroom.

So remember, on Election Day, vote Jimmy for change!

TAKE YOUR PILLS AND SHOVE THEM! – September 28

My social worker, Ms. Crane, thinks she has the right to spread lies about me to anyone who'll listen. For example, she recently decided it was her duty to inform Frankenstein, not to mention Dr. Gardner, my evil pediatrician, about my supposed tics, seizures, erratic behavior and "paranoid delusions." Gardner and Frankenstein consulted their big book of supernatural lies, *The Diagnostic and Statistical Manual of Mental Disorders*, 3rd Ed., Revised, and their voodoo manual, the *Physician's Desk Reference*, and decided to give me some new green and purple pills to keep me quiet about their evil plans. My dad came home and rattled the pill bottles in front of my face like pharmaceutical maracas. Good thing my dad,

Gardner and Frankenstein all have puny alien brains, so I can outwit them with my superior human intelligence. Instead of swallowing their poison, I hide the pills under my tongue and then secretly spit them out. I will save them all to submit as evidence at the post-alien-uprising Truth Commission hearings, when Frankenstein, Gardner and my dad will all receive the punishment they deserve for their pitiful attempts to torture and enslave me.

JUST WAR THEORY – September 30

I am a peace-loving soul who worships Mahatma Gandhi and Martin Luther King Jr.—not to mention George Clooney and Sean Penn, even though they're TOTAL WUSSES. I'm all for passive resistance and turning the other cheek and would never harm another living creature—not even one who calls me spaz, tic boy, dork, loser, monkey fag, spazoid, spaznoid or freakazoid.

Also, I would never harm Conner Richardson even though he has decided to run against me for student body president and has launched a dirty campaign in which he questions my political credentials and smears my good name.

Although I am a child of peace, there is such a thing as the Just War Theory. Have you heard of it? The Just War Theory says it's okay to wage war against evildoers. If it wasn't for the Just War Theory, right now Saddam Hussein and Adolf Hitler would be partying in the Bahamas, with the Taliban playing backup on the kettle drums. According to the Just War Theory, if you are shoved and tripped for no reason, get food thrown at you at lunch, and get teased for having mental and physical disabilities you don't even have, you are justified if some day you stand up for yourself against the perpetrators of the abuse.

In conclusion, I am committed to the path of peace and am a member of the Save the Butterflies Foundation. But let me close with a philosophical question: If Conner Richardson is evil, would it be unjust if a brick mysteriously split his head open, or if he suddenly found himself inexplicably on fire?

VICTORY IS NIGH – September 31

I hereby reject Vice Principal Chud's ruling that I am ineligible for Tuesday's class presidential election. The liar Chud says that I broke election rules and violated school policy by threatening my opponent and spreading rumors about him. Chud has even placed me on a three-day suspension in a futile attempt to suppress the truth and slow the momentum of the Jimmy Carton-mania that has swept the campus of LBJ.

It's obvious that my campaign has threatened to undermine Chud's plans to use Conner as his puppet ruler. With Conner as his lackey, Chud hopes to hypnotize us with his liberal ideology and keep us cowed until the alien uprising is upon us. It's a good thing I'm brave and not intimidated by the evil, subhuman, American-hating Chud or his weakling protégé Conner.

Have no fear, fellow students of LBJ! Keep the faith! My candidacy continues and I will obtain victory over the evil Obama-loving alien losers. Write in your vote for Jimmy Rock-Your-World Carton, and soon the drinking fountains will flow with Mountain Dew, free condoms will rain from the sky and all your acne will be miraculously cured. .

WHAT REALLY HAPPENED ON ELECTION DAY – October 5

Fellow students of LBJ, in these heady times of political change, social unrest, and voodoo economics, it's difficult to separate fact from fiction, rumor from truth. The liberal media can't be trusted—especially those brainwashed, quasi-literate hacks at the *Lyndon Baines Johnson Middle School Gazette*. But have no fear, fellow LBJ-ers. I am here to set the record straight about the coup that took place today at Lyndon Baines Johnson Middle School.

First, it has been reported that despite being suspended for misconduct, I arrived on the LBJ campus prior to first period, destroyed Conner Richardson's campaign posters and spray-painted "CONNER IS A GONER" and "VOTE CARTON OR DIE!!!" on various walls, lockers, and trophy display-case windows.

Lie number one.

Second, I have been falsely accused of illegal electioneering. Supposedly, I stood across the street from the school as the students arrived and shouted, "JIMMY CARTON WILL SAVE YOUR KIDNEYS," "CONNER IS A BED-WETTING WUSS," and other catchy slogans through a megaphone I stole from the cheer squad room.

Lie number two.

Other charges against me include trying to buy girls' votes with kisses, threatening to kill my opponent and his supporters, and attempting to stuff the ballot box.

Lies. Lies. Lies.

The most outrageous accusation against me is that I somehow snuck onto campus during the fifth-period election-results assembly. According to various versions of events, I either A) rushed the stage and tackled Conner during his acceptance speech, B) pulled the fire alarm during Conner's acceptance speech, C) used my megaphone to drown out Conner's acceptance speech with statements of fact regarding the nonhuman Vice Principal Chud and the illegitimacy of his sham election and its bogus outcome, or D) all of the above.

Already, numerous videos have appeared on the Internet that supposedly show a person who looks like me engaging in most of the acts of which I stand accused. However, careful analysis of these videos will reveal that A) they have been doctored by Chud and his eighth-grade cronies in the Audio-Visual Club or B) the person performing these brave deeds is not me but one of my thousands of devoted supporters heroically attempting to restore democracy and save the human race from impending annihilation. (Note the suspiciously monkey-like posture and gait of the "person" assisting Connor with his acceptance speech and then pulling the fire alarm.)

For the record, I herby deny all charges against me and reject the official outcome of the so-called student body president election at LBJ. I have ordered an independent review of the election results, which will confirm that I am the rightful winner and the legitimate president of LBJ.

My supporters, stay strong and never surrender! I will soon claim my rightful place. I will lead you fearlessly and save you from the evil alien fiends even if I have to burn LBJ to the ground!

THE GANG OF EVIL HATERS – October 6

This blog entry is addressed the evil cabal of school administrators, social workers, healthcare workers, teachers, and even parents who met today in room 217 to discuss my recent supposed misbehavior and psychiatric problems—namely, my threats, fights, vandalism, seizures, hallucinations, and paranoid delusions—all of which were invented by Chud and his evil co-conspirators to silence me. You are all doomed to hell for participating in this kangaroo court/inquisition. According to my mom, whom I will never forgive for her betrayal, you think "this experiment in mainstreaming has been a failure" and I need to be "some place where they can give me the structure and care that I need to thrive."

What a joke.

You are all the ones who are failures and cowards who can't deal with the truth that you are all fated to die a painful death along with the rest of humankind.

Also, according to my backstabbing mom, you all agree that Charles is an unhelpful figment of my imagination.

Another pitiful lie. Charles is real and is superior to all of you in every way because he never once lied about me, called me a liar, gave me boner-killing pills, or told me there was something wrong with me.

Guess what? There's NOTHING WRONG WITH ME!!! Instead, there's something wrong with YOU—namely, you are all EVIL and you TOTALLY SUCK!!!

SO LONG FROM SO RIGHT – October 20

Greetings former fellow-students of LBJ! By now some of you may have heard that I am no longer among you at Lyndon Baines Johnson Middle School. No, I'm not dead (you wish!). Where I am is really NONE OF YOUR FREAKING BUSINESS, is it? Some of you may have heard that I'm in juvie for exercising my right to self-defense guaranteed in a little piece of paper called the U.S. Constitution, which the San Antonio Unified School District Board of Education apparently never heard of. Others may have heard that I'm in a mental ward wearing soft clothes and popping wonder pills. Still others may have heard that I'm at some pathetic school with the word *SPECIAL* in the title.

All lies.

I can't tell you where I am, but I can tell you that a certain former U.S. vice president whose last name rhymes with "brainy" recruited me for his black ops program. So now I'm part of an elite squad doing what I do best—kicking alien butt by day and dating hot babes by night. My undercover name is So Right because every move I make is so right that my enemies fear me and the ladies can't resist me.

So... it's time to say later, losers! Enjoy your quadratic equations, your cafeteria gruel, and your childish pep rallies. Enjoy your spin the bottle, your pilfered oxycontin, and your sad little groping parties. Don't worry about me—I'll be living large with my fighter jets and my model girlfriends while you pop your zits and pray for a date to the prom. Just don't come crying to me when the aliens come to eat your livers. I warned you. You had your chance to save yourselves, but instead you mocked me. Me and Charles will be watching from the safety of a satellite circling the earth as your organs are ripped from your body one by one and devoured in front of your eyes.

Will I be laughing? No, but I won't be crying, either.

The Heart Echo

Lisa Grove

I loved sneaking out of bed at night to watch TV downstairs. Often my father would be up, and he never sent me back to bed. But sometimes, instead of an old movie or Johnny Carson, he'd be using the TV for work — heart ultrasounds on VHS tapes — and he'd watch them for hours, taking notes, making diagnoses. The hearts beat in grainy blurs of black and white. He'd turn the volume up to hear each one knock firmly, like a velvet fist, on all the doors of the body, as if warning the tenants, "I'm watching you every second, so don't act up or try to slip away." I sat there on the carpet in front of him, looking up and not understanding what he saw and heard in all the beats of all those hearts. Even when I asked, he seemed to ignore me and never explained, and I returned to bed.

But one night when I snuck down to watch TV with my father, instead of beating hearts, there were humans, standing naked and glowing white in a line, on the lip of a ditch. Surrounding them, men in uniforms. I heard no velvet knocking on doors. Only silence, thickening around my father and me and the television. I sat on the carpet in front of him and stared up at the grainy black and white picture. There were trees, dirt, the ditch, the sky. A few moments of small movements. I breathed the silence of the room into my lungs, and into my lungs I breathed the silence of the bodies falling over each other in the loose dirt of the enormous ditch, my own heart running to all the doors of my body, knocking like a maniac on my stomach and my brain, howling, "You should not have seen this. Get back to bed. You already know too much."

A Promise

Kenneth Zak

I wasn't gone more than thirty minutes, but when I got home glass was all over the hardwoods in the hallway. I heard sobbing. I ran to the bathroom doorway. It looked like a bomb had exploded. Sitting on the side of the rusty tub in a convulsing, sweaty mess was my only son – one part teen angst, one part bipolar and one part who knew. Broken mirror covered the green tile floor, the palm-treed shower curtain beneath his Doc Martens and his black-dyed mop of hair.

Blood traced his pale knuckles. He was holding a piece of mirror above his wrist and looked up to me. His bloodshot eyes looked so scared.

"Cameron! What the fuck!" I said.

In two steps I was over him. I bent down, wrapped my hand over his wrist and took the glass from his shaking hand. Man, I was so glad he let go.

"Is this what you want?" I asked.

I dropped the glass into the tub.

"I don't know," he said.

Tears and snot covered his pimpled face. He nearly slipped from my grasp when I pulled him to his feet. His sopping, sleeveless Operation Ivy T-shirt stuck to his back. We stood almost eye to eye, our faces only inches apart.

"What the fuck?" I asked.

"I'm sorry," he said. "I'm sorry."

I pulled him into the narrow hallway by his neck and pushed him toward his room.

"Come on, if this is what you want, let's go," I said.

I walked up to him and jabbed him in the chest. He backed away, nearly tripping over his black boots.

But I so wanted him to charge me. Come at me. Take his best shot.

"Come on!" I said.

What a complete, fucking idiot. I had never laid a hand on him, or him me, but I was seething. Shit, I was shaking too. I took a breath but pulled him back to the bathroom.

"You're gonna clean this up," I said.

"I will," he said. He got down on his hands and knees and started to pick up glass. I thought I knew his troubles, but he had never once self-destructed in *my* presence, not once in the sanctity of *my* house. He left that for his mother to deal with, almost as if he was protecting me or making it easy for me or trying to make me proud or be normal, whatever the hell that was, but not today. Not anymore.

I wanted to shake the demons from him, but I knelt down and hugged him. Cam's long arms held onto me like his life depended on it. But really my life did. The day he was born his reddish body was wailing, shivering and helpless. His scrawny little hand wrapped around my pinky. I recalled a promise made that day, an impossible promise to protect him.

Clasped on the floor, both of us weeping, our sweat and stench felt the same.

"I don't know what to do," I said.

His brown eyes distorted through my tears.

We rocked back and forth on the floor. Specks of glass pricked into my knees.

I wanted to fix him. I wanted to fix myself. I wanted to make all of it okay, everything. I always believed I could. What fucking lunacy.

"I don't know what to do," I whispered again, "but I've got you."

And Cam's grip tightened around my shoulders.

Borrower

Una Nichols Hynum

A hesitant knock on the door.
I look out, then down.
The neighbor's little boy,
I think his name is Christian,

stands staring at his tennis shoes,
faded T-shirt ripped at the neck.
He holds a cup tilted
at a forlorn angle,

I don't remember
what my mother sent me for,
he stammers.

Standing at the blue door
of a long life,
I can't remember either.

What did I come for?
What was it I wanted?

A Night in the City

Dave Riessen

That night, Mat, and I stayed at our aunt's house. Both of us went to bed early so we could read comics. Sometime later, the phone rang downstairs. I heard my aunt's voice outside my door.

"Lee is on the phone. Would you like to speak with her?"

"Yes."

The house was cold. I grabbed a blanket and followed her downstairs to the kitchen. The phone was mounted on the wall next to a sturdy, straight-backed wooden chair. The lights were off, but there was a candle burning in the window behind the sink.

"Hey, Sis."

"Hey, Bro. How are you doin'?"

Her voice seemed a whisper of what I was expecting. I pressed the receiver closer to my ear. "Pretty good. How are you feeling?"

"Headache's gone."

"That's good."

"What're you doing?"

"Reading comics."

"How's Osmond?"

"Okay. Mostly school."

"You got room for me to come visit?"

"You bet."

"What'll we do?"

"We'll build a tent in the parlor, you, me, and Mat. And we'll tell ghost stories."

"Soon as I get out?"

"You bet."

There was a long pause in our conversation. I listened to the clock's ticking and watched the candle's flickering light against the dark glass. I thought Lee might have dozed off and was about to say something when she spoke.

"Did you save me some Halloween candy?"

"I didn't get much."

"What'd you go as?"

"Creature of the night."

"Good costume?"

"Could've been better. Next year."

"Maybe we can go together next time."

"That would be good."

Another pause.

"One of the nurses said it might snow. Do me a favor?"

"Sure."

"I don't have a window here."

"No window? That's too bad."

"Can you go look?"

"Sure."

I put the phone down, went to the back door and looked out. Puffy snowflakes drifted lazily down through the porch's dim light.

"Does it feel like it's snowing?"

"Yeah."

"Right."

"Windy?"

"No, coming down like feathers."

"That's what I thought. I want to walk in it."

"Soon as you get out, we'll build a snowman."

"Remember Fox and the Chicken?"

"Good game," I said, thinking of us stomping the wheel shaped path into a foot of snow.

"I hope I can still run."

"What?"

"My left leg. I can't feel anything"

"Nothing?"

"No. How long has it been?"

"Over a month, for sure."

"I stopped counting. Guess what?"

"What?"

"I talked to an angel."

"Riiight."

"Last night, just like you and me are talking."

"What'd she say?"

"Said… I'd be okay."

"That's good."

"And then she showed me how to fly. I can go anywhere now."

"How?"

"My body stays here. I go away."

"How do you do that?"

"It's easy. You gotta have wings. You have to... uh oh. Gotta go. Nurse is coming. I'm not supposed to be on the phone."

"See ya, sis."

"Hey!"

"What?"

"I'm not afraid of dying anymore."

"I love you, sis."

"You, too, bro."

I hung up the phone and went back upstairs. Mat was sound asleep and I wasn't tired. Tomorrow, he would stay in Sioux City with Mom and I'd go back to Osmond with Dad. I was supposed to get back in time for Sunday dinner, but I'd miss Sunday school in the morning. In that regard it was going to be a good day.

I tried to think of what it might be like, surrounded by tubes and lights you can't turn on or off, beeping sounds for this thing or that, being away from family, waiting for time to go by, alone in a crowd, and no way to see outside?

I got out of bed, gathered my pillow and blanket, and crossed the room to the bay window. Inside the alcove, built into the wall, was a wooden seat that looked out over the street below. I pulled back the curtains, settled in and watched the snow gather beneath the distant, frozen streetlight.

a book with one page

Tina Barton

you want me to be
a book with only one page
with
large simple print
no words for the senses
descriptions non-descript
letters waxed and shined
to glisten,
to look pleasant
a few lines
of complacent sentences
full of compromise
overflowing with acquiescence
dying in surrender
one page
enclosed
tightly bound
lost in a library
of sterile shelves

But What About Moldova

Beth Goldner

Three months ago, the marketing department of my company was handed a pink slip. I'm collecting unemployment. Naseem and I don't need the money, but my father fed the system for forty-six years and went to the grave with tar-stained fingers never having taken one red cent. Somebody needs to get it for him. Our dog walker, Evan, still comes each weekday afternoon to walk Napoleon.

I haven't found it in myself to get rid of Evan.

Naseem and I have four people on our payroll: Evan; Marguerite the cleaning lady; Frank the gardener; and a man who comes to the house on Saturdays and washes our cars. I don't know his name. He is from Delaware County and is missing a few important teeth. We only have a personal car washer because he is from Naseem's motherland, and Naseem is loyal to his countrymen, especially those of slender means. My husband met him at a barbecue at his cousin's house. I won't go to the barbecues anymore. I tried to fit in, but his extended family is clan-like and, although educated and enlightened, they make it clear to me that, as a white American woman, I am a whore.

Although I would never let us actually have a nanny, we talk sometimes about having one someday. Despite two years without birth control and tests confirming that everything is in working order, there have been four miscarriages. I don't want harvested eggs or Petri dishes or Clomid or surrogates. I don't like the twist of a woman's face when she is possessed with baby lust—the rocket blast of *I must have,* the commodity nature of a child.

—We don't need a dog walker anymore, Naseem said.

—He needs the money.

—I'm sure he's got plenty of clients.

—Not enough.

—How do you know that?

—I just know.

My husband raised his eyebrows. He doesn't believe in *I just know.* He believes in evidence, double-blind studies and statistical methods.

—How can you know?

—This is his second job.

Evan cuts hair at a salon in Overbrook. He is a six-foot-five beefy man with long hair. His wrists, neck, and earlobes are adorned with diamonds, rubies, and gold, which may or may not be real. For several months I've wanted to ask Evan if he'd cut my hair. I don't believe in therapy. A hair trim every four weeks does the trick, costs less, and bypasses pharmaceuticals. A good hair stylist listens, which is what most of us really want. My current hair stylist is six months pregnant. She has ceased listening.

I was in the guest room organizing a pile of shoes when I heard a car pull up. I looked out the window and saw a Bentley parked in our driveway. I heard our front door open and I felt a little bit of pee come out. We live in the safest township on the East Coast, and all I could think was that somebody, probably a black man who is a drug dealer, had driven his pimp car up my driveway and was walking into my house with the express purpose of killing me. I was so ashamed at having this thought that I wished somebody had arrived to kill me.

—Napoleon! Evan bellowed, our Shi Zuh barking with joy.

Since I lost my job, I try not to be home when Evan is likely to arrive. If I am, I'll run upstairs to the bathroom, lock the door, and sit in the empty bathtub.

When I heard Evan leave with Napoleon, I counted to one hundred and went outside. A new Bentley is an almost-cupped hand, a slight arch with palms faced down, hood-to-hood veins of silver, and blood-red endings to alight its path. If I asked my husband for a Bentley, I think he'd buy me one. He's a physician and wouldn't be able to afford a Bentley on his salary, but he comes from old money. If I went down on him at unexpected times and in unexpected places for several months, he'd seriously consider the request. Sex has a lot of pull in our relationship. I am the second lover Naseem has ever had. The first time we made love, he thanked me afterward. It was an innocent comment in context, but I refused to speak to him for three days. *Thanking me makes me feel like a whore,* I told him. He is a grown man, speaks three languages, and is self-deprecating but confident. He ensures people's lives but in the depth of the night—and it is only in the depth of the night—if I wake up, he is always clinging to me with a neediness that I rely on.

Having money has not changed certain things for me: my back still hurts every morning, my brother is still patronizing, my parents are still dead and I am still not over it. One of Naseem and my strongest bonds is forged by the fact that we both know the gob-smack wonderment of the innocence in those who don't know what it is like to lose a parent or sibling. When Naseem was a boy, he used to sit on his rooftop with friends and cousins watching the bombs drop on his city. He was ten years old and disregarded his parents forbidding him to do this. He thought the bombings were funny. He lived a reality more real than most, but he saw destruction through a child's eyes. When he was twelve years old, his sisters were with his aunts on the other side of the city on the wrong day, when the bombs hit the right target. He will never get over it. Nor will his mother. When I think about her loss, my dislike of her—her coldness to me—lessens. His country is a place his heart will never leave, a place that owns his soul, a place I believe is the source of and cure to his pain, a spot on a map that I will never find.

I would never ask for a Bentley. I am happy with my Nissan Sentra. A part of me can stay who I was, from the lower class during childhood, to the middle of the middle during adulthood—the middle that had dental insurance but crappy dental insurance—my life that was only ten miles away and five years gone by. If Evan were my stylist, I would ask about the Bentley. An organic intimacy would have developed, the slide of fingers through my wet hair, sharpened blades in hand, and arms looming over me.

My Aunt Helen told me that when you have something important to say, practice it alone, first. *See how it sounds. Practice when you're sitting on the can.* My Aunt Helen lives in a doublewide in Port Orange, Florida. She is raising her grandchildren because my cousin is a crackhead. She does better with those kids than my wealthy neighbors do with their own. Aunt Helen's grandkids are articulate, polite. My neighbor's spawn is disrespectful and unkempt. My aunt's bathroom is cleaner than mine. Like our car washer, my Aunt Helen is missing an important tooth.

After Evan drove away in the Bentley, I sat on the toilet, peeing for what seemed like forever, staring at my plastic shower curtain that has a colorful map of the world across it. I love being in my bathroom primping. I love to floss, blow dry my hair, and apply mascara, all with the world around me. I never heard of Moldova—at least I couldn't remember having heard of Moldova—until I bought the curtain. It's sandwiched between Ukraine and Romania. I spent five minutes on the Internet and learned too much. Forty percent of its population is below absolute poverty. Their GDP is below the average of Sub-Saharan Africa. Human trafficking problems. Poorest country in Europe. I turned the computer off before finding out the infant mortality rate. I didn't want to think what it would be like to be a baby there. I stared at Moldova as I finished pissing, my voice loud and jubilant, *Evan, where in the fuck did you get the Bentley!*

Later that day I drove to the farmer's market in Merion. It was a scream of noises, fingers pointing to food, children everywhere, Amish girls selling sugary pies, and people pushing carts aggressively. I was standing at the cheese vendor when I saw a blind boy. His grandfather was leading him to a cluster of tables. The boy held a soda and sat down. He drank from the bottle, gently putting it on the table after each sip, screwing the cap back on. The cheese vendor asked if he could get me something. I shook my head *No* and moved out of the way. The boy kept drinking his soda, placing it back on the table, carefully screwing the cap back on. The two of them didn't speak and, eventually, the grandfather started dozing. I stood for ten minutes watching them. I felt a loneliness for this boy, a loneliness that he may or may not have had. Maybe the boy was quiet because he was bored. Maybe he just wanted to go home and hang out with his friends. I knew it couldn't be so. I wanted the evidence for my husband: I wanted to go sit next to the boy and talk to him, ask him if he likes his friends, ask him if his childhood is happy. Here was my baby lust.

That night Naseem and I made love and, afterward, I went in the bathroom and shut the door, peeing and staring at Moldova. I heard Naseem go downstairs. After we make love, he always does something, no matter what time it is. He gets something to eat, checks his e-mail, or watches television. Sometimes he goes for a run. He never rolls over and goes to sleep. I wish he would. I want him to need me, have me, and then sleep with nothing in between these moments. If I try to talk to him about this we'll get in a fight. He will not spend hours dissecting our relationship. We have been married for four years and we love each other in an unpredictable pattern, constantly surprised when our conversations re-engage to lengthy and intimate exchanges after weeks of rote dialogue, when our bodies revisit each other after a month of distance despite still having been making love, when tenderness pops up in front of a television after a long day. We have arguments. We forgive each other. But he is always one step away from me.

I think it was the war. I think what he lost keeps him both close to and far from me. I think he and I hold onto each other because of what we lost and the truth is that we cannot fill that gaping hole for each other. I want a baby so that I can offer something to fill that hole. But in the dusty corner of my life I have refused to acknowledge how I want to fill our lives, how those babies in Moldova must be considered, and how filling something can leave you with emptiness anyway. I turn my back to the map and whisper *Those babies* inside my head. The moment I say it aloud, I have tested it, and the moment I test it, I must say it to him. His war wasn't the only war. His dead sisters aren't the only dead sisters. My dead parents aren't the only dead parents.

Evan is paid fifty bucks each visit to do the following: Walk Napoleon one block down Beidler Road, turn right onto Henderson Road for three blocks, another right onto Canyon Run Drive for four winding blocks leading back to our house. Make sure he shits, scoop the shit. Then he gives Napoleon three biscuits, refills the water bowl, and puts one cup of kibble in the food dish.

Every weekday since the Bentley had appeared, I sat fully clothed in the unfilled bathtub reading *The Washington Post* between noon and 1:00 P.M. I'd hear Evan enter the house, greet Napoleon, and soon thereafter leave for their walk. Then I'd go downstairs to look at the Bentley. Sometimes the windows were halfway down, and I'd put my nose to the opening, careful not to set off the alarm, and sniff the new car smell. Once I took pictures of the car at every angle. One day I smelled the slightest hint of cigar smoke.

—I'm here, Evan.

I had decided to be in the kitchen when he arrived that day, baking cookies. He grinned with surprise.

—Day off. Cookies, I said offering the plate up.

He took a cookie, bit, and then closed his eyes and gave a low growl of satisfaction. He fed a small piece to Napoleon, who was in frenzy.

—Any big plans?

I looked at him, confused.

—Your day off? Any big plans?

Choose, I thought. I almost said shopping but while I was committing to this word, shaping it with my husband in mind, trying to make him proud, my mind went back to Moldova and then Moldova attached itself to shopping and that there was a brand of watch whose name rhymes with Moldova, with a price tag more than a Moldovan's yearly income.

—Are you okay?

He touched my shoulder.

After he left, I stood in front of the bathroom mirror, pulled a large chunk of hair from the front of my hairline, held it flat against my forehead, and put a strip of masking tape across the hair just above my eyebrows. I took scissors and I cut.

The next day when Evan arrived I announced myself again from the kitchen, where I was polishing silver. Evan walked in holding Napoleon, and he quickly recovered from a look of confusion. A dog walker doesn't ask a client why her habits changed, let alone why she is polishing silver, let alone why she has crooked bangs.

—Busy day for you? I asked with a strained chipperness.

I am a lousy conversationalist in my own home. When I'm with my Aunt Helen and my cousins in Florida, I am a big talker. The mobile home is too small for all of her grandkids and two dogs. Everybody talks, everybody talks loud, nobody can hear anybody.

Evan looked at me, his face half-buried Napoleon's neck.

—Pretty average kind of busy, he said.

I touched my uneven hair and considered talking with Evan about Moldova, a manageable topic. I didn't want to talk any bigger, not Darfur or Somalia or Sierra Leone or unpopular conflicts, not how the Palestinians can sometimes be right and the Israelis can be sometimes be wrong and unpopular opinions, HIV in Russia and China and acceptable silences, why we are an obese nation, why we do nothing about the pothole on Bryn Mawr Avenue near the Shirley Bernard bridal shop, a pothole that keeps eating the tires of my car.

Evan arrived early one morning, and I was in the laundry room folding towels.

—I'm pregnant, I announced, walking into the kitchen before he could even say hello.

I had taken three over-the-counter pregnancy tests the day before. I had not told Naseem. Evan looked at me and broke into a wide grin. I had not hidden in the tub for several weeks. Evan had finally stopped looking at me curiously, but he had not asked why I was home. He did not ask me if he was no longer needed. He is my dog walker, and he had not commented that, with a few careful snips, my bangs could make their way toward being less crooked.

—Congratulations. Wonderful, wonderful. When are you due?

—Can't count on a due date. I keep losing them, I said with a shrug.

Evan looked at me, really looked at me, for the first time since we met. If he were my hair stylist, he would have already heard about the babies lost. He would have heard my resigned and tempered tone, telling him I know it will happen, that a baby will happen. I would not discuss this in a skittish voice, that I-have-to-convince-myself-it-will-happen anxious voice that my privileged peers clamber through yoga and therapy and body fat measurements and ovulation schedules, trying to get their husband aroused because if he doesn't fuck her that very day, they may not have children. I would tell Evan that I don't want my child conceived in a desperate fuck with my husband. Evan would know that I would not perceive these miscarriages as my body's failure or Naseem's failure or any other white American whore's failure.

Napoleon started to whine. He wanted me to hold him. He did this each time I got pregnant. Evan clasped the leash to Napoleon's neck.

—Wanna join us?

We walked outside. It was too hot for May, the atmosphere a heavy soup. Napoleon peed himself before he got to a tree. He was excited to have both of us.

—Nice car, I said, as we pass the Bentley.

—Yeah, she's a beauty.

We veered off course and walked four blocks down Caley Road, which led us to Valley Forge Road. We took a right and I left Evan in charge of the walk, but I was not sure if it was him or me who pushed the wooden piece on the Ouija board of our lives.

—What do you think of Moldova?

Evan pondered the question for a moment.

—Is that a cabernet or a merlot?

—No, Moldova the country.

—Okay, well, I have to tell you, I didn't even know the country existed.

I waited.

—Let me guess where it is.

—Sure, I said.

—Middle East?

—Nope.

—Europe?

—Yup. Eastern Bloc.

Evan shook his head. We were almost back to the house, the Bentley in full view.

—So, how long have you known where Moldova is? he asked.

He began a warm chuckle as he smoothed his hand along the roof of the Bentley, and I didn't know if he was laughing at me or in delight of his sleek machinery.

My husband discovers things by touch. He placed his hand on the side of my neck this morning when we were making love.

I imagined there was something unique about the way my blood pulsed through my artery that told him I was pregnant. I didn't know if this ability was why he was a doctor or what happened after years of being one.

—You're pregnant, he whispered.

He held his hand on my neck, his body slowing to a gentle rhythm. He was not mad at me for keeping it from him. I wanted to take his hand, with both of us naked, the three of us, really, a family, and go into the bathroom. I wanted to put his hand on my still-flat, wet belly with something inside so inconceivably perfect and loved already, and I wanted to point at the countries on the map, show him Togo, the Maldives, Yemen, and Kiribati.

The next day I joined Evan for Napoleon's walk.

—I'm starting to think about names.

—Are you going to name him after your husband's family—give him an ethnic name? I don't remember what country your husband is from. I'm not so good with knowing about countries.

—Who said I'm having a boy?

—I dunno. I always imagine that foreign men who are married to Americans only have baby boys. Isn't that strange?

—No. Not really.

I looked down at Napoleon. He was sniffing at the grass.

—Will you cut my hair?

Evan looked at me, twirling a ruby or fake-ruby pinky ring, smiling a smile that may not have been a smile but a desperate attempt to figure out how to say No. He had seen my crooked bangs and did not offer his services. But I thought it was a Yes-smile he was giving me.

I thought that Naseem and I will keep making love during the pregnancy, which will feel wonderful. It will make me happy for my husband and remind me of our abiding love, but it will scare my heart. The baby will bridge us, maybe, just another centimeter. I will fear for our child, what I won't be able to give him, what Naseem's family will. I will not be able to stop thinking about blind boys, about how not wanting something is worse than wanting something and not getting it. And in this dream I ask Evan what he thinks of my hair, if it's beautiful, if he wants to touch it and reassure me that the babies in Moldova will survive, not go skyward to a Heaven where my parents and Naseem's sisters are. I hold this dream as a map of the world across my neck, Naseem's hand resting across its topography.

At the Diner

Nicole Vollrath

The day you pawn your vintage watch, you find yourself at the diner. The booth squishes and sighs as you climb in, farting under the weight of your massive butt. The sound doesn't make you feel like ingesting calories, but your stomach gurgles and it's what Paul wants.

Menus are wedged between the condiment holder and the wall. Paul takes one and starts reading like you aren't even there. Like he lacks the common courtesy to take two and hand you one, even though you're paying. You are always paying.

You get your own damn menu. It's sticky, of course. Everything is sticky. Your thighs on the Naugahyde. The flesh beneath your too-tight bra. Fat squeeze bottles of ketchup, mustard that you'll overuse in silence, making every penny count.

Paul puts his menu back against the wall. He always orders the basic breakfast: two eggs, sunny side up, sausage and white toast he'll jab into the yolks. He'll twist the corner of the bread and slurp the yellow goo like a fox in a henhouse. "Mmm. Chicken embryo," he'll say.

It seemed original the first dozen times. Like, who looks at an egg that way except a nonconformist, a philosopher, an unappreciated artist with hip, post-modern sensibilities? Janet actually described him that way, seeing "post-modern sensibilities" in that greasy skater cap he wears and his service station jacket with "Chump" sewn on the breast.

You agreed. You couldn't believe a guy that cool wanted to bang you. Regularly.

Now you'd like to ask Janet if fighting the line at the food bank is post-modern. Is it "po-mo" to sleep on a musty mattress above his brother's garage, sneak Tupperware into all-you-can-eat pizza night, and go a year without washing the truck because it'll just get dirty again? Is it "po-mo" to lose your job at Hot Topic for crying in the dressing room? To have your credit cards suspended and sleep through GED test prep? Is it "po-mo" to gain sixty pounds in three months? For nothing to make you happy but food? For food not to make you happy at all?

You'd like to ask Janet if Paul's songs about driving to Encinitas to bang his ex-girlfriend are "po-mo," too. But Janet's not around to ask.

The waitress comes by with coffee. You turn your cup up like a reflex. In the old days everyone drank coffee because it stretched out your stay. You spent all night laughing at your parents, renaming the band and planning what to do with all the money fame would bring.

You stir in half and half and pour the sugar "hobo style." As if it's got to last you awhile.

"What time is it?" Paul asks, like he's got someplace better to be.

Raise your empty wrist, white as a scar.

"I wish I had a beer," Paul says.

In your head, words form: I could leave. I could leave.

Where would you go?

Your voice drags itself up your throat, dry from disuse. "It's good to want something."

Paul's eyes meet yours for the first time today. Your stomach growls.

Five Stars

Monika Zobel

The kitchen towel absorbs the sweat
of steamed beans, blood from the calf's flank.
Into the gravy boat I pour *every bed is a grave.*

I used to lie in yours while you shoveled
flour in my mouth. Love was measured in the cup
of your hand strangling mine. One more
spoon of salt and I would have dried.

You rubbed chili powder on my lips
after slipping by accident
in a pool of rum and mint.

I chewed cucumbers for their lack of spice.

I knew someday my head would spill
like the watermelon you cracked
when you choked on hidden seeds.

I didn't water the ones you sowed.

I have no use for marinated tongues
or eyes flushed with Tabasco drops.
I need to taste the water in my soup.

The Egg

Sandy Robertson

The rain was light but relentless, hanging veils of grey between the dispensary and where she stood in the long line of women. We're not moving, she thought. She braced her shoulders against the fatigue for a moment; then resumed her former slump to keep the cold slivers of water from entering her collar and running down her back. If we could just swing our arms around, or jump up and down, she thought, I'd get warm. Turning her head, she saw the guard, immobile as a statue, standing under the eave of the barracks. No, she thought, just stand still; don't make trouble. Not today.

How long had it been since she'd seen an egg? Mentally ticking off the days and weeks, she arrived at months. It has to be six months, at least—no, wait, longer. It's early October now, and the last one was before Easter. Not that Easter had mattered here, the Japanese didn't recognize it; the Chinese didn't either. Most of the other foreigners in the camp had taken no notice; only the missionaries had made a fuss—old Mrs. De Vries and her god-awful hymns. But today; no one's going to care about today, she thought, except Annie and me. The line jolted forward; then stopped. And Robbie.

Where's Robbie right now, she wondered. Does he remember? Tears seeped out, blending into the wetness on her face. Of course, he'll remember. Annie's fourth birthday—he'll be thinking of her now, feeling this same rain on his face. Or maybe he's working inside the mine today, dry, but in darkness. She shuffled forward, mud sucking her shoes. It's been so long since we've seen each other, but, sure, he's remembering that last birthday, before we knew the Japanese had taken Shanghai. Such a lovely party: the table set with pink linen and colored hats; the big white cake Fu had baked and carried triumphantly into the dining room through the swinging door, three yellow candles blazing, to set before little Annie's widening eyes. This cake's not going to look like that, she thought. Nothing like that, but at least she'll have one. What's a birthday without cake?

The rain was coming down harder, colder, but now she could see the dark outlines of the dispensary emerging ahead. Maybe it's not true, about the egg, she thought. Maybe someone heard wrong. I really mustn't count on it. Rumors raced like lightning through the camp all the time: the Americans are finally retaliating in the Philippines, Swedish freighters are getting permission to dock in Shanghai, soon they'll start transporting internees back across the seas. After nearly a year, she knew not to pay too much attention to them. In the end, nobody ever really knows anything. But when she'd heard this morning that they were handing out eggs, her heart soared: she knew just what she was going to do with hers. She pictured Annie's little fingers stuffing cake, sweet and crumbly, into her cheeks setting off bursts of goodness inside her mouth like nothing else in her young memory. Or would Annie remember Fu's cake? Fu's fragrant, Western-style cake, his first one. He'd been so proud.

She was soaked now, cold wet to the marrow of her bones. Wish I hadn't sung happy birthday to her, she thought. I've set her up—now she knows it's a special day, a day just for her. But what if it's not; what if it's just like all the others? Will she ask me? When I kiss her goodnight, what will I say? Goodnight sweet pea, little peanut, I'll say, like always. Mrs. De Vries will be listening on the other side of the blanket hanging between our cots, like always. So much for privacy. Will Annie cry? I can't bear it if she cries, I can't; I can't bear it.

A quick tug on her sleeve made her look up. There she was, Mrs. De Vries, on her way back to the barracks. Her ruddy face was split into a broad smile; her eyes glistened merrily through the mist: Margaret, she said, holding an egg up for her to see. Then she was gone.

Margaret felt a wave of joy spread through her body, bringing her alive. She straightened her shoulders, raised her chest and let the rain fall onto her face, into her mouth and even down her neck. Hah! She was going to make this day happy for Annie; she was going to make Annie smile, Annie laugh, they were going to laugh together, the sounds gurgling in their throats, ballooning out and reaching the rafters. Soon even Mrs. De Vries would start chuckling, then the other women, then their children, unable—any of them—to resist the infection of gaiety, the rumblings of laughter growing and washing over them all, then over the blank stone faces of the guards outside, rising up like a huge tidal wave, filling the camp, breaking free and spilling across the road to the men's quarters, then down deep into the mines, illuminating the dank interiors, before exploding into the sky, scattering showers of happiness far and wide, falling on all of them, falling across all Shanghai—no, all of China.

The line moved again, and Margaret stepped up to the open window. Now she too was holding an egg. Cupping its small weight in her hand, she stepped deftly among ruts and wet muck, careful not to slip, not to fall, not to drop this prize before she got to the tiny stash of sugar, the rusty tin of rice flour, the hoardings of so many other days that had been waiting for a day such as this. Because you never know, she thought, when a day such as this can happen; you just never know.

Obligingly, by the time she got to the camp kitchen, the rain had stopped. A weak sun began to warm a corner of the sky. She emptied the scant handful of sugar into a bowl, picked up the treasured egg, kissed it, and cracked it sharply on the rim, holding it up to release its contents with a soft plop. Then the back of her hand banged against the bowl, her shoulders sank, her legs turned thin and spindly beneath her. She grabbed for the edge of the table, her eyes swimming with the image staring back at her from the bottom of the bowl: an eye in the bloody glob, a tiny beak and feathers forming in the dark gooey mess.

She heard Annie's feet then, clattering up the wooden steps, bursting into the kitchen. Mommy, mommy, where are you? Is it time for my birthday, Mommy? Leaning against the table, she turned and looked down into excited, round eyes, an upturned face, a small mouth open in anticipation.

Happy birthday, sweetheart—she kissed the mouth again and again. That's right, it's your birthday. You are four years old today. Isn't that wonderful? Happy birthday, baby.

A Dinner of Import

Justin Hudnall

The young couple at the table next to mine was having a Dinner of Import. She was young, he had started graying at the temples, but love will be love and I've always preferred my men with dignity. Dignity comes with age.

They'd sat down and perused the menu with some tension, ordered on the waiter's first pass. Then, as soon as they handed up their menus, she leaned forward.

"Why did you bring me here? What did you want to talk about?"

He couldn't help himself. He smiled. Then, with just mouthful of words, she was screaming with joy. She didn't care how nice of a restaurant it was. She was out of her chair, kissing him and squealing all in the higher tones.

He tried to shoosh her, but his heart wasn't really in it. They were in love and no one should seem annoyed by that. Especially when dining alone. It's just unbecoming.

"Congratulations on the happy day," I said when she caught my eye.

"My wife," the man said, squeezing the girl close to him and rolling his eyes in relief. "I thought she would never die."

How to Cannibalize Your Dead

Peter Hepburn

Dice up your dad's thyroid then toss
in the cartilage, arteries, goop, and veins.
Use a ten-gallon pot like you're fixing
a chicken stew, a big burgoo made

with onion, tomato, and corn. Cut off
your mom's lemon zest hair, and scalp.
Cover in rum run straight from a keg.
Gurgle, ripple, and guzzle that glob

until chunks go limp and lumps melt down
to liquid ecstasy. Season the mixture
with saccharine gestures and fenugreek.
Stir and shake the primordial soup.

Go clockwise at first. Swirl in your whorl,
your codes, your labels, your marks, and scars.
Spin in reverse like a Whirling Dervish.
Grab your griddle and sauté some DNA

then crumble in those delicious bones.
Lower your burner and turn down the prattle
of ghosts that babble like oatmeal gone lava.
Serve with Irish Stout and beamish tongue.

Just Half Way

Kyra Freeburg

So there I was just half way in the bag, not in the fifth of scotch way either. I was half way into an old letter carrier's mail bag when it occurred to me things could go terribly wrong. I can remember that my dimly lit pubescent brain had no more time to think past that thought. I was flanked by one older sister and one younger sister "helping," and I use that term ever so loosely here, me into the mail bag. We were timing ourselves to see who could get into the canvas bag fastest. The sticking point here was we were teenagers, gawky, long and lean. Imagine trying to jam an octopus in an envelope. Our chosen tool for this competition was unremarkable, a large regulation letter carrier's canvas mail bag. Where it came from originally I'm not sure. It was one of the many odd treasures we found in our basement. It was our prop for this day's amusement, which was born out of our fight against boredom. We were a house of five girls, teasing; temptation and torture were always a means to pass the time. Preying on each other's moments of weakness and turning it into a joke was high art in our house.

I was first to try, whether by volunteering or by being talked into it. I knew if I squeezed my lanky teenage frame into that oblong sack, I would get my sisters laughing. That generally was enough for me. My sister's laughter was always inclusive, it strung us together. It was our language. We started out this event in our circa 1970's living room. The living room, complete with gold marbled carpet, an autumn brocade European style sofa and long flowing pale drapes pulled back from the picture window with elaborate gold braids and tassels, all of which reeked of my dad's filter-less Lucky Strikes. The fact we started out in the living room is a significant point to note because the living room's a private, indoor, safe location. It's away from the prying eyes of our quarter-acre-lot-suburban-neighbors. My believing the living room was safe, well, unfortunately that assumption was woefully miscalculated.

My sisters seemed overly eager to help me ensconce myself into that mail bag. Their long fingered hands pushed at me, positioning me into a semi-fetus type ball. They tugged at the canvas bag roughly trying to get it to cover as much prime real estate as possible. I was successful in relinquishing my natural spine curvature in order to achieve my goal of getting in the bag. Now in the bag, I breathed in a moldy dampness that reminded me of our basement. The smells of old socks, wet wood and laundry detergent pressed in around me. I wasn't claustrophobic; I tend to like small spaces. The summer I moved into my closet to avoid sharing a room with my sister proved that. My cheek was pressed against my fuzzy warm thigh as I thought, "Okay, now I've done it." But, as this thought crossed my mind I felt the sack cinch up. I heard the maniacal cackling of my sisters–and then, there was movement.

Something had gone awry. I felt myself travel from the frictioned surface of the living room carpet to the smooth cool linoleum of the hall. I had gone into the sack head first, I was slumped back with my chin to my chest and knees brought up high. My shoulders were the surface on which I was traveling, experiencing my changing world. I started to bark my protests, but had trouble keeping laughter out of my voice. That changed when I heard the large wooden front door swing open and the screen door squeak. Oh no, oh no, I pleaded, less laughter, more mortification, as I realized where this was leading. I was dragged, like yesterday's laundry, out onto the small, cold, cement porch then gently down a step or two pausing only a moment before my journey continued across the front lawn. The surprising loud whoosh of the grass under my head and shoulders blocked my thoughts as I traveled over the nubby surface. Then we stopped.

I ended up cinched tight in a mail bag rolling around our small manicured front lawn. I heard my sisters footsteps recede as I desperately tried to expel myself from my canvas womb. Their laughter was near hysterical as they moved away and I heard the front door slam. The rumble of a car passing by brought me to the knife's edge of teenage embarrassment. I lay there slightly stunned as what to do next. Escape was first in mind, but only from my shins down was sticking out of the bag. I looked like a demented lollipop. With what little movement I had, I slowly walked my fingers down to my shins. I needed to find the clasp for the cinched rope that held me tight in a little spastic bundle. I was sweating now. Between the smell of the sack and my regurgitated air, I was reluctant to take deep breaths. My fingers twisted around the metal clasp searching for the release mechanism. I prayed I was not attracting an audience. I strained to listen for snickering or murmurs from the imaginary crowd that had formed in my head. This crowd now consisted of frowning teachers, beauty queen neighbors and cafeteria crushes all shaking their heads and rolling their eyes. Their lifted shoulder shrugs in "What more do you expect?" Their gestures stung me as my sweaty fingers cramped around the clasp. I pulled hard at it, and at the same time I inadvertently had taken in a large breath of the fetid bag air which proceeded to coat the insides of my mouth with grit and decay.

At this expenditure of paranoid energy, sweat and spit, the clasp finally released and loosened the tension on the rope. I arched my back as I rolled again to maneuver my release. With this next wriggle and roll I unfolded out onto the sweet smelling grass of the lawn. My face pressed deep into the cool dark soil before I flopped over and kicked away the bag. There I lay looking up at the pale blue sky, white clouds, panting, like a Pekingese. Luckily, no massive crowd had gathered on the sidewalk, there was no one standing there pointing at me as I had imagined. I stood and took a furtive look to see how many neighbors were perched on their front steps sipping Lipton ice tea to enjoy the show. I saw none, but this was the type of neighborhood where neighbors watched such goings on from behind pale lace panels. I turned from my scan of the houses across the street to see my sisters red faced and laughing behind the huge living room picture window. I'm sure they fully enjoyed the show from that vantage point. Picking up the mail bag, I jogged up to the front door, all the while shaking my finger at them in my best, "I'll get you, you dirty rat" gesture. I stood there waiting as they unbolted and unlocked the heavy front door. Then they let me in, as they always do. They let me in with their laughter, their love and their treachery.

O'Parrot

Randy Herman

To whom it may concern by Wallace J.

I am so sorry I flipped your mattress and found all that treasure when you were at the opera probably which don't worry I am going to give it a nice home. Including your golden goose parrot, ha ha. Too bad I figured out what it is made out of. Too bad I can live forever with trees around me and pay the rent for all time off that stupid bird. Oh well, have a nice life.

Which reminds me, your bird keeps staring at me. Now I know why you stick it under that mattress because that is what you have to do with problem stupid birds that just stare at you and they are so conceited and they think they know everything. So if you ever want to see your stupid bird again, you have to give me all your worldly goods, what is left of them. Also you have to give me all your money or five hundred dollars whichever is more and your stupid bird is watching me so hurry up and take this idiot off my hands so I can be rich behind my wildest dreams and if I don't hear from you by six o'clock tonight you can kiss Mr. Feather Brains goodbye, I don't care if I don't get the money because I am a man of principality.

But because I like you, you don't have to give me everything you own, but I still expect all that money.

But for one day only I pay the tax, so two hundred dollars and we are even which means I will leave parrot breath on your porch tonight and the money better be there which I am not going to give you the exact time because I am not stupid, I don't care what that bird says. Anyway she is a little crazy, I am beginning to think, because all she does is laugh at me.

So I expect at least one hundred dollars if not more and that stupid bird is making me crazy also. What is your problem, bird? Probably if I smash it, it won't even break probably because who knows what it is made out of something poisonous or even lead which I am thinking of suing you for all of my distressedness.

So you take this stupid bird and this bag of quarters. It is all that I have. Also I will leave my bike if twenty-seven dollars is not enough. I am sorry I borrowed most of your house but I am returning everything unused mostly and if you will accept this offer of good will then I will not pursue legal action and it will take a few trips, but I will bring your bird on the first one, don't you worry.

If you do not take the bird off my hands, then…Okay, I am willing to walk your dog and mow the grass also and I will pay you for my time if that will help, but not less than four dollars per hour. That is my final offer. All right: Nine.

Yours truly, Wallace J.

Craigslist

(a found poem from personal ads)

Charlie Daly

I can't afford batteries anymore.

I thought i'd give this craigslist thing a shot.
Call it a booty call if you want.
I am just craving that something thats unfortunatley
lacking in my life
RIGHT NOW
LOVE DOESN'T SEEM TO BE LOOKING 4 ME

Suggest we hop in the car and head out to a remote
motel,
since my kids are gone until Monday.
NO STRINGS
NO BS

I am Looking for a man with Herpes,
possibly more.
MUST be
over 21,
LATINO,
a MARINE.
I'm not going to take a chance with some druggie.

I want dirty drunk sex in a truck, I don't have time for
a relationship.

Hold me.
Thrill me.
KISS me.

I'll pay of course,
What kind of woman would I be if I didn't?

Florentino

Mark Radoff

Cousin Florentino drove a dented green Chevelle station wagon with a magnetic Jesus and Mary perched comfortably on his dashboard. Jesus' outstretched arms would have poked Mary right in the face had she not been kneeling next to him. Over time, her magnetic base weakened and Mary slipped from the top of the dashboard, coming to rest by the Philco radio dial whenever Florentino accelerated quickly or made a sharp turn.

As a general rule Florentino drove no faster than thirty-five miles an hour, even on the Pomona freeway. He'd lug onto the Pomona interchange with Jesus perched in the best spot, and Mary sliding somewhere between the tuner and the ashtray making it impossible to smoke or turn down the radio. Fortunately he didn't smoke, so Mary spent most of her time sitting perpendicular to the ashtray panel while Florentino switched between Spanish folk music and Dodger games.

My brother Anthony and I occasionally spent weekends with Florentino and his wife Leticia, while our mother went to Mass and our father to the synagogue. Neither of us was particularly clear on our consanguinity to Florentino and Leticia, leaving us to piece together our mother's unsolicited clues on our own. "It's complicated," she would start…which we translated to mean that: (a) we were not cousins; (b) that someone had an affair; or (c) she just didn't know. Since our mother never explained anything in one sitting from beginning to end, and rarely in full, we learned how to speculate at an early age.

To us a cousin was akin to an arranged friendship coupled with a biological imperative. Cousins came over to play and your dad sent all the kids to the backyard to "get to know each other better," whether you liked it or not, while adults drank beer and someone tried to borrow money. Cousins did not drive light green 1960's station wagons with the Lord God's only son elbowing virgins into an ashtray and forcing her to listen to spring training baseball games.

Physically Florentino was set heavy, some might say fat. He favored immodest T-shirts that made no secret of his navel or lower belly. The two most memorable things about him were his laugh and his dog. Florentino had the sweetest laugh we'd ever heard. High, smooth and sincere. It sounded exactly like one of those Chattanooga train whistles right before it went into the tunnel. And he thought everything was funny. Everything. It was impossible not to laugh along with him...except when Busch was around.

Busch was a pound mutt that Florentino rescued from two simultaneous predicaments, homelessness and poverty. Having met Busch halfway, and offered his backyard as a refuge, Florentino expected Busch's indiscriminant gratitude. A patient, submissive and grateful ward who longed for the chance to lick a stranger's face. Nothing more. That's what we knew of small dogs, and expected nothing less when we saw his bushy little frame in the backyard. What we did not anticipate was the generosity of his teeth or his disdain for clichés. And as bad as his bark was—it sounded like someone swallowing a gravel driveway—his bite was far superior.

By necessity, Anthony and I kept our distance while Busch sharpened his overbite on the chain-link fence, spending most of our time inside surrounded by an ensemble of knickknacks and figurines that covered every square inch of furniture and counter space. This was a different type of danger. Leticia had an eye for clutter and left no space unoccupied. Three inch high ceramic angels, basset hounds and clowns crowded the mantle while rosary beads connected and unyielding variety of crucifixions. The crosses were spaced evenly over household surface areas like breadcrumbs in the woods, but too many sprinkled to ever find your way home. Everything was breakable so we kept our distance.

Inside we pretended that their couch was a football end zone, and that I was the only defender who could stop Anthony as he hurdled (airborne) over the cushions for six points. As in, most football games we only got three or four chances before we were banished to the other end of the field, which in this case was the city park, down the street.

One particular weekend we spent "Good Saturday" at Florentino and Leticia's, planning to meet our parents the next day,

Easter Sunday. Florentino woke us up and just said, "Let's go for a ride." The three of us crowded side by side in the front seat of the station wagon. Leticia had already left for Mass while we slept in.

Florentino crawled onto the freeway, testing the horn and patience of every driver in or adjacent to the slow lane. Thirty-five miles is a tough way to make friends in Los Angeles, and he didn't... at least not while he was driving.

Miles before our exit, Florentino, Jesus, Anthony, Mary and I pulled off the freeway and drove down a side street. We drove past discount stores, bail bondsmen, taquerias and pawnshops, until we finally came to a real neighborhood. Florentino pulled into a park, driving slower than usual around the lot and stopped under a large tree. Then we just sat there.

"What are we doing?" I asked.

"Yeah, why are we here?" Anthony always copied whatever I said.

Florentino just laughed. "Hee, Hee, Hee. We're just resting." He *actually* laughed like that!

"Resting from what? I insisted.

"Just wait," he told us. Then he pushed the seat back (which was the only direction it could go), leaned where the headrest should have been and closed his eyes.

Not surprisingly, the park was empty. It *was* Sunday.

Still we sat.

We waited longer than any ten or eleven year-old boys could be expected to last until finally another car drove up. A woman pulled up to the other end of the parking lot, opened her trunk and walked toward the closest picnic table. She was dressed as if she'd just left church—which was probably true, since this was Easter. Florentino grabbed both our shirts and pulled us out of sight. I concluded the obvious...that this woman knew Leticia and if she saw Florentino she would tell Leticia that he hadn't gone to the late service as he promised.

We watched her walk slowly around the park bending over from time to time, seeming to drop things as she went along. As she got closer to us we could see her hands were filled with chocolates, eggs and candies that she tithed to the trees, bushes and grass in the park. Meticulously, she covered the grounds, careful to conceal the largest chocolate bunnies in obscure, un-obvious places.

She returned to her car, lifting an oversized green box from her trunk, and walked right toward Florentino's station wagon. We took the bomb-shelter drop position beneath the dashboard as she walked by, complete with hands on the back of our necks. If it worked when the Soviets came, it could work in any situation. Florentino, who had no chance or interest in hiding on such short notice, simply pretended he was asleep. The Chocolate Woman walked right in front of our car while we did our best spy imitation: peering through the space under Jesus' wrist, we saw her put a giant chocolate and cream rooster into the hollow of the large tree next to the station wagon.

Then she left, leaving us to wonder and wait. Florentino still pretended he was asleep which would have been believable, except with this much chocolate around. But he wouldn't get up, and he wouldn't let us out.

Not much later, two vanloads of children, with creased pants, pastel dresses and polished shoes arrived and lined up at the park entrance. Florentino pushed us out of the car and told us to go.

We did as we were told and walked toward the group, slowly at first, then at a run. Anthony and I didn't know anyone, but just got in line, putting one foot over the other, hoping to hide our Adidas.

As the Easter hunt began every child made a running start. Everyone except us...because we alone knew where the eggs were hidden. Slowly we surveyed the park, feigning surprise and amazement as we extricated the biggest treasures. We cornered every single marshmallow-filled-rabbit and creamed egg, navigating the minefield of vinegar-dyed hard-boiled eggs resting in the overgrown grass.

To both our surprise, the Chocolate Woman announced that no one had found the grand prize...the *GIANT ROOSTER*. Children scattered and pushed each other looking under hedges, bushes, in culverts, *even* on the lawn where the hard-boiled eggs had been hidden! But they didn't look in the hollow of the tree by Florentino's car, which is exactly where Anthony and I were headed. Slowly, with our cramped arms burdened by bounty, we made our pilgrimage toward the *ROOSTER*.

The anti-climax of the moment for us was easily outweighed by our knowledge that we had just recovered enough chocolate to last us until Labor Day. That is, until we got back in the front seat and discovered that we had to split everything with Florentino.

"No way. I'm not breaking off the head."

"Yeah, no way." Anthony said.

"You have to start somewhere. Hee, Hee, Hee."

"Yeah, but the head's the best part," I protested.

"That's what people say who don't know where to begin," he told us, as he started to unwrap the *ROOSTER*.

Reluctantly we broke the *ROOSTER'S* creamy head off as we eased back onto the freeway. Listening to everyone honk at us as we wiped the extra cream off on our Levis...I can't remember chocolate ever tasting that good.

Tire Tracks

Meredith Kunsa

Mom's hand rests on a '49 Ford coupe
with balloon-sized whitewall tires.
A hat is slung over her right eye.
The car's front fenders surge forward
like GIs assaulting a beach.
There's a fancy spotlight mounted
at the driver's door like a jeweled
hairpin above an ear.

Mom loves her cars, sometimes
she just sits at the wheel, a Lucky Strike
dangling out the window. Other times,
she slams out the front door, leaves
tire tracks in the street.

My favorite car is the one my stepdad
bought her as a gift for leaving the guy
she'd run off with. A powder blue
'52 Studebaker convertible buffed
to a California sheen. It has plastic
seat covers and a body wrapped
in chrome with custom skirts that flow
over the rear wheels. Like all her other
cars, this one is in top running order.

Fatherland

Patrick McMahon

So this is Torrance. This flat, sprawling suburb twenty miles straight south of West Hollywood, just inland from Redondo Beach, creates a stark contrast to the luxuriant Ranchos Palos Verdes peninsula just to its south. It strikes me as an endless expanse of apartment complexes, small homes and strip malls, all bland, more of them run down than kept up. I sit in a diner, maps and photos and documents spread out, recalling a similar diner with a similar spread on the north side of Chicago only a year ago. Then I was exploring the neighborhood in which my birth mother was born. Today, I'm exploring the neighborhood in which my birth father died.

"Hot open-faced turkey sandwich with mashed potatoes and gravy, please. Does that come with cranberry sauce?" All the information I need is right here, on his death certificate, the one obtained last year with the help of Dick the genealogist, Scott's friend in San Francisco. I stare out the window as the names echo. Scott and Dick in San Francisco. My friend Scott is about the same age as my brother Scott, who I haven't met. My acquaintance Dick is about the same age as my birth father Dick, who I will never meet.

The server chings the tip of the glass as she refills my iced tea. I'm relieved to see her name is not Lori or Barb and turn my attention to all the locations listed on the death certificate: usual residence, place of death, employer, location of injury, crematory. All the addresses are in the LA area. They are all places I could visit to try to connect with something of him. His death is listed as a homicide, so there must also be a police report, and probably an autopsy.

Today's agenda includes finding the "usual residence," "location of injury," and maybe the crematory in Laguna Beach. I wish the plans to meet his brother Jack hadn't been postponed. It would have been nice to have his story before this expedition.

I feel very much alone today. I've told no one I'm doing this and feel like a detective out on a limb, or like a moth sensing the flame. Strange, this compulsion to visit all these sites. Seems to me most people would think it morbid or pathetic or obsessive. The only person I know who gets some of this is my old friend Alice, whose dad died when she was two. Last year when she opened up to me about him, she told me she became compelled to visit the hospital he died in. And she would occasionally visit his grave. Dick has no grave. His ashes, as well as his side of the story are at the bottom of the ocean off Laguna Beach.

I finish my iced tea, pack up and head out. With little trouble I find the Anza Victoria Apartments and park near the entrance along a six-lane, busy thoroughfare. With traffic whizzing by, I sit and take it in.

It would appear he had some style. This place stands out among most that I've seen in Torrance. It's a large, modern, Spanish style, gated complex of three-story buildings. It looks well kept with lush landscaping and large trees, a place that would have been attractive to me when I was living in apartment complexes in the early eighties, which is when he lived here. Barb told me he always had a nice place to live, which rung a chime in me. Even as a struggling, full-time student at San Francisco State, I lived for two years in a beautiful 100-year-old Victorian flat, and one year in a brand new three-level townhouse.

A little self-conscious, excited and apprehensive, I walk the length of the sprawling cluster of buildings fortressed by a black, wrought-iron fence. I cross the street to take a couple of photos, one including my truck. Documentation. Back by the main entrance, I stand and wonder which building his apartment is in. Just where is #159? I envision him walking this same sidewalk, punching in a code, and it's not long before I want inside. Standing out here is not enough. Not by a long shot. I want to find apartment #159.

Calling on last year's detective skills and imagined tactics of Robert Ludlum's spies, I consider calling the rental office to look at an apartment. Maybe even #159, since there's no name listed by it and might well be vacant. No, too complicated, and if they show me a different apartment, it'll be a waste of time. I'm not sure I could maintain composure. So for fifteen minutes, I stand and fidget and attempt to look like I'm waiting for a friend to come let me in, when finally an unsuspecting accomplice swings open the gate.

Reaching for a look that says,"Oh, thanks. I just buzzed someone," I slip through and walk like I know where I'm going.

I'm good at directions, addresses, maps, finding places quickly. It's a left-brain approach, rather than intuitive, maybe similar to what Dick did as a black jack dealer in Vegas. It's not long before I figure out the layout and find #159 and am slowly approaching the door and suddenly wondering what in the world I'm doing here.

I stroll by and glance through the vertical blinds. Yes, it's vacant. I walk back and peer inside. Yet another nice, basic beige apartment. Only this one is as bare as the looted stores on Melrose Avenue after the riots. There's no sign of life. Like all other paths on the trail of Dick Shields. Emotions begin to rumble, and I scope out a place to sit. I just want to be here for a little while. Can I do that? Can't I do that? Will someone come along and kick me out?

Stairs across the lush courtyard become my viewing perch. I sit in the warm sun, relax, inhale the sweet scent of blooming flowers and stare at the door of #159. My father lived here. The man whose seed created me and according to Barb, the man who would not parent me. Richard Ransom Shields. I feel like he's holding a part of me ransom with so much unknown, unresolvable. I imagine him living here, after the divorce from his second wife. I imagine the apartment with furniture in it, him watching TV, sleeping in the bedroom, cooking in the kitchen. Did he cook? I'd guess not. Did he sit and read? Is this where he printed his philosophical 'sayings' on parchment paper which I now have copies of? Was he friendly with neighbors? Did he have people over for dinner? Did he have parties, one-night stands, a steady girlfriend?

I can feel the dam beginning to crack as I pull out my only photo of him that clearly shows his face. I imagine him coming home late from bartending at The Den, his place of employment listed on the death certificate. I recall my stint in bartending school in 1983, compelled to pursue this as a means of extra income to save money for music school while working as an engineer. My bartending father died the same year I took up his trade. I recall staying at the Flamingo Hilton in Las Vegas on business that same year, and recently learning he worked there as a blackjack dealer in the late sixties and early seventies. Psychic and physical paths crossing. My gaze wanders back to #159 after glancing at someone walking through the courtyard who gives me no notice.

My father lived in this apartment and one night he didn't come home from the Den. One night, the one before his 46th birthday, according to Barb, he went to a party and got into fight trying to get a party-crasher to leave. I hear her words again, "He fell or was pushed down some stairs, hit his head, and lay in a coma in a hospital for six weeks before dying." As I sit wondering if this is the truth—and then whether it matters or not—my thoughts and feelings about this man stir some more.

I feel sad about never knowing him. I feel angry that I will never get to face him. Because deep down, even though I've heard so much about it from Barb, I want to hear from him why he gave me up. I want to hear from him why he would not be my dad. I want to see his face when he tells me. The face everyone says is so similar to mine. I want to hear his voice telling his story in his words. I want to know what he smelled like, how it would have felt as a kid to sit on his lap or tug at his shirt.

As everything around me disappears except his photo and his apartment, I realize I want more. I need more. I have to somehow come to terms with his life, his choices, his death. Maybe if I could look into his eyes and come to some sense of him. Any sense at all. Would he be distant, ambivalent or loving? I want to know if he ever thought about me, if he ever told anyone about me. I want him to know what happened because of his actions. I want to see his face when I tell him about my other father, the one who chose to parent me, who tried his hardest, but found his capacity to do so limited by alcoholism. I want to see him dealing with me being gay. I want to look deeply into his eyes and ask, "How could you give up three of us? Did you want *any* of your five children?"

I sit quietly on the stairs as this scene pulses in my head, envelops me, and my heart beats faster. I begin to sweat.

I pick up my camera and just as I discreetly snap a few photos of the apartment and the area, a next-door neighbor comes out and walks by his door. The Asian woman with two small children reminds me Dick's second wife is Asian and makes me wonder what it would have been like to find half-Asian half-siblings. By the time

I wonder how long the neighbor has lived here, if maybe it's been nine years, if maybe she knew him, she's gone. I wonder about other neighbors and the managers. Is there even one person living here who knew him at all? I suddenly want to search for that person, hear them say,"Oh yeah, I remember Dick. A real nice guy." Or, "Oh yeah, he was kinda quiet, kept to himself." Or maybe, "Oh yeah, he was a real jerk. Kept late hours, made lots of noise." Anything. Anything at all.

But by this time, my eyes are moist, my lips are quivering, my heart is gaining weight, and it's all I can do to sit here just a little bit longer.

A couple more people walk by his door. Seeing normal, everyday life going on slowly places Dick Shields into it. He was a resident here, a human being who breathed and lived and slept like all these other people are doing now. He was just a person living a life like everyone else. He was not even one of the fantasies I had about him. He was who he was. No more, no less. And so, somehow, he becomes a little less of a ghost as a tear trails down my cheek.

I imagine Lori sitting next to me, and sharing this experience with her. I wonder what she'd say. I think of my two other adopted siblings out there somewhere. I wonder if they know they're adopted, if either has or is searching, and imagine the surprise they have in store if they do find their mother: a brother who's already done it. What if one of them found Barb before I did, knew all the things I'm learning, had already sat where I'm sitting? Perhaps one day one of them will sit here. And perhaps a neighbor will notice how several people have come to stare at apartment #159. Perhaps someone will notice this mysterious pilgrimage to an empty shrine. This thought produces a surprising chortle.

And on this note, in this state, chuckling to myself in a dazed and confused way, the way people laugh when they've been through enough, the way they laugh when they finally find humor at the bottom of the barrel, I amble out of the Anza Victoria Apartments, back to my truck, and sit inside.

I can't stop thinking about this image, all of Dick Shields' kids gathered outside #159. This scene becomes more and more humorous, and I begin to laugh out loud. I laugh until the convulsions sink down to my belly, where all the pain begins to mix in. Soon all five of us are sitting on the stairs, viewing his apartment, comparing stories, perhaps all chanting something like:

> Dick.
> Oh, Dick.
> We're all here now.
> Can you see us?
> All your children.
> We're here.
> To pay homage to you.
> Curse you,
> Forgive you,
> Haunt you, or is it the other way around?
> Maybe we'll give up.
> Confrontation null and void.

And then we do a chorus line instead of understanding.

Reasons for Smoking

David Tuffy

If I smoked, I would have sat this week on the top of the stairs leading to my apartment, wearing my blue jeans and a thin, white, cotton T-shirt. I would have felt the bite in the air of these first fall evenings and the splintered wooden steps under my bare feet as I looked out at the streetlights casting their circles into the darkness along the sidewalk.

I would have thought of you and watched the smoke curl through my fingers then rise up and disappear into the sky, felt it fill my lungs with each deep drag, held it for a moment and then released it in long breaths, enjoying the buzz, ignoring the ashy taste coating my tongue and the back of my throat. The damp, clear and threateningly present smell of early autumn would be dulled by the smoke, but not enough to block the sense of urgency it always brings.

I would have sat and smoked and stared for a long time into the neighborhood's night sky, the sounds of car tires on the blacktop and of pedestrians living out their lives loudly on their cell phones not breaking my reverie. I would have sat and smoked, unmoving, until forced by the hard plank underneath me to shift position and this would have been each night of my week and it would have felt normal, but I don't smoke and it didn't. It didn't feel normal at all.

Renunciation

Tracy Darling

You need to give up alcohol said my therapist
But I've already given up so much I answered
Well you need to give up more she countered
you don't want to be a victim to anything anymore, don't want to rely
on anything but yourself
Oh, but that's just it, I said, I can rely on alcohol
'cause it is there for me every time I need it
an always and forever 'til death do us part kind of thing
and alcohol is consistent
same look, same taste, same
feel as I wrap my hands around the
glass, and the best part, the same feeling
every time warmth in my heart after the first swallow, smile
in my eyes after the first glass, and after the second glass
a tingling in my body
alcohol gives me everything my husband does not, it is reliable
and consistent, warm, touches me
in lonely places, I don't think I could ask for anything more
and you are asking too much
for me to give up one more thing
I already gave up blaming him for my misery
gave up my guilt and melancholy, and I have yet to gain anything
higher or greater or spiritual so I say no more, no more
I say someone give me something
even if it's just a drink

Ploughman

Nickolas Furr

Somewhere overhead, flies buzzed and a hawk called. Tall grass swayed in the breeze, tickling his face and arms. He breathed raggedly, open-mouthed, the only human sound around. Beyond the smell of blood and death, the scent of wheat still lingered, drifting to his nose, his mind. The smell of good earth and green grass: it was the smell of life to a ploughman.

He touched again the blade that pinned him to the earth. Slick with oil and his own blood, it had resisted his attempts to pull it from his belly. He'd lacerated his fingers trying; now he was too weak to do anything but try to push it away.

He had never meant to be a soldier. He'd never wanted to wear the leather for his king, never wanted to go into battle with an axe in hand. An axe was meant for trees and stumps. It wasn't meant to be used on another. His axe was steel and oak, and lay just out of reach. He had always planned to use it until the grave, never knowing how close that would be.

His king had called him, and he, a man of the plough, had come.

The king was not a bad man. He taxed his subjects at the same rate. It was steep, but it was fair. The taxes paid for the wardens who patrolled the lands, the roads that carried the goods, the priests in the city, the walls of the stronghold, and the men that stood upon them. They paid the price of civilization.

They paid the price of protection.

Never before had the king called on his subjects to stand and fight, to pay the price. He had called them all—ploughmen, smiths, tinkers, greengrocers. They had come. He had left his plough sitting in the field, his mules standing in the stalls.

His son, Jed, could reach the plough handles, but he was still too small to control it. Sharlotte would have to hire a man to work the fields that he had worked since he was a boy. She would do so, even though she would grieve the loss of her husband in battle. She would never know that he waited for an army that did not come.

She would never know that he had fallen, not to the soldiers of an invading army, but to something worse.

She would never know that his life was taken by heroes.

He lifted his head, trying to find his axe. He reached for it, unable to touch the wooden haft. Stretching, yearning, his fingers fell short again and again. Exhausted, his head fell back to the earth. Coughing, blood spat from his mouth, alighting on his chin and neck, joining that which was already there.

A tyrant, one of his fellows had said. From over the horizon, an army rode toward us, and they believed our king to be a tyrant. Taxing his people wrongly, imprisoning his people in the gaols below the stronghold; our king was a tyrant whose reign needed to end.

Yes, there were men and women in the gaols—people who deserved to be there. Bandits and thieves, murderers and drunkards: these sorts were held to task for their crimes. Had he been king, had he been born to rule and not to plough, he would have done the same.

Yet he was no tyrant.

He lay still, wishing he had brought his cutting knife with him to the battle that had never come. A knife in his hand would have ended the pain quicker than the sword that was doing it.

This blade would be his epitaph. No words would be spoken over it.

No one made any noise, save for the insects and the birds. The others had died during the night. Those few that had lasted until morning had coughed, cried and prayed, but all were silent before the sun rose to noon.

The ones who survived, those few had run. He would have run, had he been able to. But he had fallen early to a man in mail, a man who drove him to the ground and left his blade inside him. Heroes fought not for king or country or coin, but for an idea. That their king should die and so should all who tried to stop the heroes—that was an idea.

He and the others had arranged themselves in ragged lines, watching the horizon, waiting for the army to come from the north. None of them knew who would sit on the throne if the king were gone, but all of them would fight to keep him there. They were not warriors, but they were men of honor, men of the earth, their king's men.

As boys, they often dreamt of fighting for honor and king. Jed did, with his friends. Holding sticks like swords and axes, they played at war, but it was only play. Like his father, Jed's hands would callous from the plough handles, not from weapons he would choose not to wield. He would never be a warrior. He would never be a hero.

The heroes had come, seemingly, from nowhere. At one moment, it was only the king's men, watching and waiting. A moment later, a dozen or so men appeared, cutting into them, opening chests and bellies, taking heads from shoulders. The heroes bristled with weapons—swords and poleaxes, bows and crossbows, some things he had never seen. The man in mail who had left him pinned to the ground had drawn another blade from off his back and cut open the neck of the smith who had spoken of tyrants.

It was over as quickly as it had started. Those that couldn't run lay on the grass and joined their fellows in death. Cursed, or blessed, with a few more hours of life, he had sweated through the night, weighed down by the leather, unable to free himself. He didn't sweat now, now that he was cold.

He raised his chin, straining to look back over his head at the sun. It was descending to the west. Nightfall would soon arrive, and like all ploughmen, he would close his eyes with the coming darkness.

For a moment, sunlight glinted off his axe's unstained blade. He smiled and reached once more. Turning his body, forcing the sword deeper into him, he stretched and found the handle. He wrapped his calloused fingers around it, pulling it to him.

Strength gone, he sank back to the earth, gripping the axe, but unable to lift it. Cold and exhausted, he closed his eyes.

This is not a weapon. It is the tool of a ploughman. In a just world, this would become my son's.

He pulled the axe as close to his chest as he could, pressing the oak and steel against him.

Sharlotte, my wife, I should never have left. I should never have taken the leather and left the plough in the field. I should never have left you my widow or my son without a father. I will pass with your face in my gaze.

I dream of a place where we see each other again, where we can watch our son play. I dream of a place where an axe is only a tool, where the earth is rich and moist, where the grass is green and sweet, and the harvest is bountiful.

I dream of a place with no heroes…

Somewhere overhead, flies buzzed and a hawk called.

以心伝心

isshin denshin

Gina Barnard

to communicate by spirit—to imply

Only because
of *isshin denshin*
do I let you leave—wordless—
through the front door without
a bite, without a kiss.

"I know why you're mad"
I whisper

as I mince garlic,
so small, ever small,
the smell yellows my eyes.

Simple Math

Shawna Smart

It ain't no Nine-to-Five, this thing I do, in the glass-glittered alleys and vacant industrial lots of the city. My stare bores into Jake, the fight hustler, as I wipe my mouth with a filthy hand. One more fight and I can take the money and go.

Drink, shower, forget.

Fuck, I need that drink now.

The first four haven't been too bad, but I am feeling the strain. My inner thighs are trembling, my skin is crawling up the back of my eyes and every bone in my body is aching.

His glance reminds me that I can skip this if I let him share my bed. Mine reminds him he's too old to wake up a eunuch.

The crowd begins to whisper and I detect a note of anxiety in the sound. I shift my eyes to the circle as the last fighter steps in.

She's a ragged vision, tiny Asian china doll with a ragged sweater and immaculate porcelain wrists. Her thin, determined face is pale, dominated by dark almond eyes.

The spectators sigh, their hard shiny eyes shying from her tiny form to my thick one. I shake my head as I hold up a hand, shooting Jake a venomous look.

This is a fucking child.

I stare at Jake, but he avoids my furious eyes. He won't pay me if I don't. When you are a drunk, the math is simple.

The girl flows into the ring and her movement whispers to me. I feel the hair on the back of my neck ripple and stir. She is poised and liquid, her approach predatory.

I nod at her; she bows and assumes a horse stance.

Ah, her bow is fractional. She believes she is superior; I am curious myself.

A blink later, a whisper of air whines as it chases the flicker of her black cottoned leg. Her blurred foot appears in my left peripheral and vanishes again.

I feel my nose break.

Damn, she has something. Third time this year I've had my nose broken and by a slip of a girl too. I feel my lip curl in a reluctant, appreciative smile, as her slight form weaves around me, light as a dandelion. I shift to defense as I scrape my streaming eyes with a quick sleeve.

What you got there for me, baby?

She rises in a trophy kick that would be applause worthy in an exhibition. I block her kick with a casual forearm, clench my hands around her airborne ankle, and give it a hard yank.

Too bad she's in the real. Someday, if she survives, she will be good, but not tonight.

I don't want to hurt her, but I got to have that drink.

I swing her high off the ground and her soaring kick turns into the frightened arm-waving flutter of a helpless child as I curve her up, around and down, slamming her face first into the gravel littered dirt.

The impact wrenches a shriek from her lips and the crowd flinches along with me in unwelcome synchronicity.

A black silence falls in both my inner and outer worlds. A violent surge of shame almost doubles me over and I fold my arms across my belly to hold it in. There is a breathless period when no one moves or speaks. All simply stare.

A single tear slips down the slack of her jaw from a trembling eyelid, transforming the dusty powder of lot dirt into a muddy trail. The overhead light traces the fine peach fuzz of her cheek with glints of amber fire. A small river of blood, black in the night air, is spilling down her temple and pattering the gravel below.

The delicate blue of the skin under her eyes looks so fragile, I want to vomit.

Her fight pimp eases up, eyes prying at my shame-numbed face. He leans forward, whispers a single word next to my cheek.

"Cash."

I smile at him, a tight glittering row of vicious blood-streaked white; he flinches, prudent instinct overriding greed.

Too late.

I roundhouse Mr. Fight Pimp on the side of his pointed little head and he sags to the ground unconscious. I lean over him and spit with heartfelt contempt into his rubbery face.

Then I relieve him of his fat wallet and make it disappear.

"Fuck your cash!" I hiss.

Jake is holding out my prize money.

I snatch it from him.

He shrugs at me as he backs away, holding his hands up in the air. I see most of the crowd has wandered away; none of them look excited anymore. Plenty look sick.

I turn to the girl and lift her to her feet. She manages to stand alone after a moment spent clinging to my arm, her face a white blur in my shadow. I dab at a trickle of blood running in a thin thread from one of her nostrils with one of my sleeves and stuff a twenty in her front pocket

"Get something to eat, little cobra."

I feel her dazed eyes follow the back of my head as I turn away.

Behind me, Jake is pawing through the fight pimp's pockets in a feverish haste, exclaiming over the dope he finds, a cascade of gold chains already stashed in his underwear.

Gritting my teeth, I pin my nose between my palms and wrench it back into place, as fresh blood, snot and tears run down my chin. Stuffing the money in my bra, I pull out a cigarette and light up.

The glowing cherry of my smoke shivers in my jiving fingers as I head down the alley toward the strip.

I'll get a fleabag for a night or two, one with a hot shower, lots of ice packs, and order-in Italian.

First the liquor store.

I need two bottles. One for me and one for eternity; it's gonna be forever before I forget that child's face.

Coupled

Angie Vorhies

then a couple
of kids

we were
related

not by blood
but by kiss

by kin
and kind

by law
united

until
by tears

divided

now, be gone
by bygone

and I be-
come

your first wife,
once-removed.

The Captive

Linda Boltman

I could hear the rhythmical drops of blood fall from the ceiling. Steadily, one, two, three. I watched, almost transfixed, as they fell on my right arm, where they momentarily caught, tangled in the fine, blonde hair, then gathered and slid slowly down the side of my arm onto the floor.

My wrists ached from the tight rope wrapped back and forth between them, digging coarsely into the area closest to the bone. I could see the chafed, torn skin on either side of the rope, red and brutally ugly.

It looks like a bad cut of fresh meat at the grocery store, I mused. A thick, almost clear liquid oozed from the center. *I wonder why it doesn't bleed more?*

I can't focus on that, I thought to myself, shifting my eyes from my wrists back to the dropping blood. I tried to count the number of drops and stopped at forty-six.

I wondered how long I had been hanging here. I'd blacked out after the attack and when I awoke, I was hanging by my wrists from the ceiling, my feet barely touching the floor, in a dank, stone basement. It appeared I was alone. For a long time, I'd listened intently for any sound from the dark corners, but for hours now, I'd only heard the steady dripping of blood from a wooden plank above my head.

I tried to shift my weight. My left foot was becoming numb. The ball of my left foot had been carrying the majority of my weight against the cold, damp floor. There was a smell, a nasty smell, I couldn't place. The smell of death sounded too dramatic, but was the only description that came to mind.

My temples ached. I leaned my head back and closed my eyes, but the extra weight it put on my wrists caused me to flinch. I tried to clear my thoughts. I couldn't die here. I wasn't going to let myself die here.

I wondered about the blood. *Was it human? Was that the prior victim above me and would it soon be my blood dripping down on the next victim?*

My body tensed. *What was that?* I could hear a slight shuffling of feet above me, followed by what seemed to be a scuffling sound. It was quiet for a moment broken only by quick, strange muted noises before I heard the shuffling feet again, followed by a slow, dragging sound. The drops of blood above me quickened, then began to slow as the dragging sound moved further away. Within minutes, the sound and the dripping blood had ceased and I was enveloped in silence.

Was that a body? Perhaps he'd come back and moved the body. That's what the dragging sound had been. He was dragging the body out of the building! Oh, dear God, does that mean he'll come back for me next?

I felt tears well up in my eyes and angrily willed them away. I had to keep my senses. I had to stay strong. I was only beaten when I gave up. I had to do what I could to stay alive and I had to outsmart this person if I was going to do that.

I heard footsteps behind me and an old wooden door open and close. I remained still. I allowed my body to go limp and silenced the screams of fear and pain within me. I had to pretend to be unconscious.

I waited. The tension built. Strangely enough, the initial pain of the tight rope against my wrists dulled into almost numbness. I continued to remain still. I could outwait him.

Ultimately, I heard the footsteps approach. I felt cold hands on my body, pulling me up. I remained limp. Cold fingers moved against my wrist, feeling for a pulse. I focused on my breathing, willing my body to breathe, my heart to slow.

"Better not be dead yet." I felt hot breath against my cheek. "I've got plans for you, little girl. I want to see your face. The whole joy is seeing the expression on your face as you die."

The cold arms grasped my body once again and pulled me up with one arm to release the pressure on my wrists. I could hear him cutting the rope above me with what sounded like a large knife. I waited for the knife to cut through, then allowed my arms to drop in front of me and let my body go limp.

"Jesus, woman! You're dead weight!" I could hear the knife drop to the floor in front of me as he caught me with both arms.

Within an instant, I gathered every ounce of strength within me, fell to the ground and in one motion grabbed the knife, turned, and with both bound wrists, plunged it into his stomach and again into his heart.

The look of complete surprise on his face as his knees fell to the ground in front of me was followed by a look of confusion as he fell to the floor. I could see what he meant. The whole joy is seeing the expression on their face as they die.

Father Figure

Aurielle Destiche

In my rear view mirror I see you
standing behind my car. On your right
the front yard of wirey grass and dandelion puffs
I used to wish upon. To your left
a plum tree that grows from a spot of green
but no longer bears fruit.

I look ahead to the wooden garage door.
Nine years ago I watched the headlights
of my mother's Buick expand as she backed out of
the driveway.
I cried, not because she was leaving,
not because I thought she might never come back,
but because I couldn't blame her.

You stand in my rear view mirror.
Your wife gone. Your son gone.
And still your arms crossed
your expression unchanged.

Without looking down, I put the car in reverse-
my foot on the gas.

Fire Season

Janet Tait

The winds changed everything.

In Southern California, the Santa Ana winds sweep in from the desert in the late fall, bringing with them the hottest, driest weather of the year.

In October 2003 the winds fanned a signal fire set by a lost hunter into a blaze, dubbed the "Cedar Fire," that killed fifteen people and destroyed 2,232 homes. I had seen the flames from our house in Rancho Bernardo, their northernmost finger a blazing threat on the hillside barely a mile away.

The fire never reached us.

Now, on an evening in October 2007, the Santa Ana winds had kicked up again. With the winds and the heat came the fires. The "Witch Fire" in North County. The "Harris Fire" near the border.

In the living room of our small, recently remodeled house I huddled in a recliner, sipping a Coke. I told myself this was just another fire. Another in the list of local disasters that touched other people.

My husband John leaned forward in his leather chair, searching through the TV channels for new information, like a hunter after the rarest prey. His black hair was flattened to his forehead from the heat.

He stopped on a local news show. Residents east of us were evacuating– cramming suitcases, overstuffed paper bags, groceries, pets and children into minivans and sedans.

The reporters kept repeating the same information: don't worry, if you're ordered to evacuate, you'll receive a reverse-9-1-1 call; the fire is miles away, it won't reach Rancho Bernardo until tomorrow, if ever.

I turned to John. "We should pack something. Just in case."

"We should. But what?"

I had no idea. Clothes for a few days? My favorite books? Vital papers? Half of our possessions were in boxes, the rest scattered as we finished installing new hardwood floors, bought new furniture and built our dream kitchen. Boxes and bags were stacked high in every room. We owned so much ... stuff.

So we packed nothing.

My eighty-year old mother lived a mile down the road in her condo. Her memory was failing. She had a dozen medications for a long list of major medical conditions.

John's mom, Peggy, and his brother, David, also lived in Rancho Bernardo. Peggy was as old as my mother. David, on Social Security disability, might not be much help in a crisis.

If the fire reached us, we might have to evacuate all of them as well as ourselves.

Later that evening, we took refuge in the home theater to sleep. The room's sound-insulating panels muted outside noise, so we barely heard the hollow, empty shriek of the wind and the constant scratching of tree branches against the house. Still, memories of the last fire season stirred a fluttering deep inside my stomach that would not subside.

Around 1 A.M. I dozed off. A little after 4:00 John shook me awake.

"Get up. We need to go. Right now."

"What? Why...."

"R.B. is being evacuated."

I jumped up and followed him down the hall. "They said the fire wouldn't get here until tomorrow!"

"Guess they were wrong."

"What do we take? Passports? Birth certificates?" I said.

"I don't know. Forget it, we can replace them."

We ran to the bedroom. I glanced out the sliding glass door. The wind brought smoke billowing through the backyard.

Smoke? How did the fire get so close?

John threw a suitcase on the bed and started piling clothes in. I picked out my best jewelry and tossed it inside.

In the backyard huge sparks were plummeting into the grass.

Oh my god, it's here. The fire's here.

"We have to go! Now." I pointed to the sparks.

John slammed the suitcase shut.

"I'll get your mom and meet you at the evacuation center." He hauled the case to the front door.

"What about Peggy?" I grabbed my purse and ran for the garage. "I can go—"

"David can help her. Or I'll go back for her."

As I stepped inside the garage the heat threatened to smother me. I pushed the opener and the door rose.

It was the end of the world.

The wind whipped into the garage like a tempest. The air was filled with bugs of all kinds: enormous black beetles, brown moths, broken-winged butterflies, spiders ripped from their webs. Birds dipped and flew through the windstorm, trying to keep aloft. Smoke gusted in so thick I could barely breathe.

Across the street, my neighbor Jeff's house was silhouetted against an undulating wall of fire. The wind churned the smoke and sparks through his home and as I watched the crackling flames consumed his green door, his tall palm trees, his picture window.

The stench of burning wood and leaves assaulted me. Everywhere I looked something was on fire; the big pine cattycorner from our house, the red tile roof of the new custom ranch house two doors down.

I'm not going to get out alive.

Across the lawn, John had reached his BMW. I could hardly see him through the smoke, but I stopped to watch him throw the case in the trunk and turn to look at me. There was a stillness at my core, an acknowledgement that this moment might be our last together.

"Love you. Be careful," I said.

"I'll see you at the evac center," he said.

Yes, yes, oh God, please.

I slid into my Camry. My hands shook as I put the key in the ignition. One step at a time. Turn the key. Put the car in reverse. Switch on the headlights. Back out.

I glanced up. *Shit, oh shit. The roof is on fire.*

One of the tiles on our wood shake roof was burning. The flames flickered with the wind, then spread to another tile, the dry wood fibers curling into black cinders as the fire consumed them.

The house is gone. Nothing will save it. Drive, just drive. All that matters is getting out alive.

I spun out into the street. The smoke was so thick, I could see only a little way down the road.

My world narrowed to just those few feet. I drove by memory alone. *This* is the length of Cloudesly Drive. *This* is how far to drive until the turn. The sole light was the fire reaching into the sky to my right.

After an eternity I burst out into the intersection of Pomerado Drive and headed to the freeway. The air was clearer here; I could see for ten, maybe fifteen feet. I began to be aware of things around me again; other cars, the pounding of my heart, police lights flashing. Three cruisers sat on the meridian by the I-15 entrance.

What were the cops doing sitting here? Why weren't they helping us evacuate? Driving through the neighborhood, sirens screaming, knocking on doors ... anything!

We'd gotten no warning the fire was so close. The reverse-9-1-1 system hadn't worked. We escaped because John couldn't sleep and had noticed the evacuation order scroll by on the TV.

I'd seen other cars as I drove down the street. More people might still be asleep in their homes. Jeff and his family, my other neighbors ...

Why weren't the police doing *anything?*

My hands shook so much I could barely guide my car onto the freeway without crashing. Did John get out? I should have gotten my mother, not him.

Driving along in the slow lane, I hit voice dial on my phone for my sister in Berkeley. The shelter would be slammed with evacuees. I could do something useful; ask her to call around and get us a hotel room. I had no idea how long we'd need a place to stay.

The clock in my car read 4:40 A.M. on October 22nd, and this year's fires had just begun to burn.

Bardo

Aurielle Destiche

If this world doesn't turn you on I will kiss you
enchanted with my wine stained mouth. Light
bursts color content, graded running hues hurting to
use my body. Turret star storms, elevated,
uneven, flesh against yours. There's no life beating
around us.

We are new.
Backward and shy, there was a time before we were
born when we were all made alive.

The grass soughed when I fell in as dwindling sun-
heat rose, bringing your scent with it,
twirling around till shrub-showers couldn't wash your
smell from my hair.
You super-ignited my landscape and I, I ran through
the sunken garden behind your eyes.
Flowers ticked tongue beats; the petals moaned your
name in the after-dark foliage, scarred
and carefully groomed.

I stole the life from between your legs and hid it
between mine transcending in wonder and dread.

In this space we are infinite.

The Yellow Cup

Scott Barbour

The day I shot my dad started like any other day. I lay on my back with my hands folded in an X across my chest and watched the gray light seep in through the blinds. I tried to stay on the surface but the downward pull was too strong, like a whirlpool swirling in my chest and through the bed, the floor, and the foundation—a black funnel cloud sucking my heart deep into the earth.

I got up and pulled on my boots and went outside. A smudge of red-orange sky glowed above the snow-covered lot across the street. The air was still, silent, too early for traffic or even birds. My breaths came out white. I walked to the street, my feet crunching on the frozen ground, bare trees sticking their black branches over the sidewalk.

Trashcans lined the curb on both sides of the street—huge, plastic, dark brown, with handles designed to fit the trucks that would come later to empty them. I tried to take a stroll and clear my mind, but I couldn't ignore them, each one stuffed full of the waste of one family—meat wrappers, potato skins, soup cans—everything that's left over from living. Bread crusts, orange rinds, mayonnaise jars.

All that trash got me thinking about where all that food had gone, into the bodies of my neighbors, churned into shit and piss that was flushed down into the sewer. We walk around up here thinking we're clean and separate from one another—better than one another—and the whole time, below our feet, all of our shit and piss and bloody tampons and used rubbers are mixing together. Because really we're all the same, and that's what we are in the end.

When I stepped in the back door, my dad was in the kitchen in his short-sleeved plaid dress shirt and tie. He stood with all the lights on staring at the black coffee maker. My dad was a little overweight and needed a haircut. His dark gray hair covered his ears and his shirt collar in back. His bushy mustache would've looked sexy if he was gay and it was 1974.

"You're crying," he said. There was no surprise in his voice, no question, no judgment. Just a statement of fact, tinged with concern.

"No, I'm not," I said and wiped my face with the sleeves of my jacket as I walked down the hall to my bedroom. I was sweating under my arms even though my hands were numb.

I closed the door, but it popped back open. My dad stood in the doorway staring at me.

"What?" I said.

"Are you thinking about hurting yourself?"

"Get out of my room. Ever heard of privacy?"

"Answer the question. Are you thinking about hurting yourself?"

"No—I'm thinking about hurting you."

"I'm calling Dr. Stiegler."

"No! I'm fine." I stared up at him, hoping to convince him I didn't need a shrink, but I had to look away pretty fast and focus on my Hubble Telescope poster on the wall, a blooming purple and green galaxy shaped like a monstrous ear floating in the void.

"Show me your arms."

I pulled up my sleeves and showed him my healed scars, thin white lines from various shallow cuts.

My dad grabbed my left elbow and ran his fingers slowly over the bumps. There were no fresh cuts. He left the room, went into the bathroom, and came back a minute later with pills in one hand and my blue plastic water cup in the other. I always used the blue cup. His was red. My mom's was yellow. They sat lined up on the counter by the sink. Red, yellow, blue. Even after my mom was gone her cup sat there for weeks, also her toothbrush in the rack; both of them seemed to get crustier the longer they sat there. The yellow cup got a white film around the lip from not being moistened by my mom's mouth.

People think it's the big things that get you—the empty chair at Thanksgiving, the extra car in the driveway—but it's not. It's the little things that sneak up on you and surprise you, like the flaky white film on a yellow plastic drinking cup. I kept looking at it every day when I brushed my teeth, until one day, a couple months ago, it was gone.

"I'll be checking your cheeks," my dad said, his way of telling me to swallow my pills.

"What did you do with the cup?"

"What cup?"

I glared into his eyes. In the dim light, the irises looked black. "Did you just throw it away?"

He was quiet for a few seconds. I could see him thinking about what I said, trying to put it together. Then his shoulders slumped and he pushed his hand toward me.

I took the pills from his palm, satisfied I'd made my point.

I hadn't taken my medication for a few days, even though it helps. When I take the pills I don't cry as much and the thoughts don't come as often—the stepping in front of trains and off bridges. But the side effects are cruel for a guy. On the pills, I can get a hard-on like normal but no orgasm. How's a young man supposed to not be depressed in a situation like that? Still, a useless boner is better than the ward. I took the pills, swallowed them, and let my dad gaze into my opened mouth.

"I'll fix you some eggs."

"I already ate."

"Don't lie to me."

"Why would I lie about that?"

My dad stared at me. We both knew. It was all covered in the therapy. The loss of appetite, pushing people away, lying for no reason.

My dad went into the kitchen, and I heard him rattling the pots and pans.

I knew I'd have to go sit there and shove some eggs and toast in my mouth just to get him to back off. The thought of it made my head throb and brought the taste of vomit to my mouth.

I sat at my desk and stared out my window. Between our house and the neighbor's I could see a few feet of the sidewalk, one and a half trashcans. I remembered how I used to watch for Mitch from there in the mornings. That feeling when I'd catch sight of him passing by on his way up the driveway. The rush in my chest.

He tried. He really did.

He even came to the funeral, looking solemn in a long-sleeved shirt and blue tie that didn't match his brown pants. He kept coming by before school, hanging out on weekends. He pretended there was nothing weird about me wearing jeans and flannel shirts in summer, sitting on the bank fully clothed while the other guys stripped and dove in the quarry. But he couldn't take it for long.

It's the constant dreariness that gets them. The worst sin of the clinically depressed is our failure to fake it. When people say "How are you?" we want to say "Fine, how are you?" like any other screwed up member of society. But the words won't come. We're more likely to moan or sigh. People think we're not trying. But when the world is just a collection of objects competing to be the best noose-holder, it's hard to force a grin.

There was that day at McDonald's. I didn't realize until later that Mitch had made a special deal of it. Taking me to McDonald's on a Saturday and buying me lunch.

"I probably won't be able to hang out with you much," he said, before taking a bite of his Big Mac.

He had a girlfriend, our mutual friend Denise. "She's, like, 'You never spend time with me,'" he said.

He was going out for the soccer team. His classes were getting harder. AP.

I chewed my food and stared at him. He had sandy blond hair with one big lock that fell across his forehead each time he leaned forward to take a bite. When he sat back up to chew, he jerked his head to get it out of his way.

He had a job bagging groceries after school. His mom was making him do tons of chores around the house. He had to start thinking about college.

I stuck a French fry in my mouth and chewed it. "Soccer, huh?" I said.

It wasn't until later that night that I realized what had happened—that he'd dumped me as a friend.

"Breakfast," my dad said.

I went to the kitchen and sat down at the chair. My dad sat across from me with his coffee. There we were, the two of us.

After my mom, there was a kind of silence in the house I'd never heard before. A silence that seems like it's not the silence before something, like it's just going to go on and on. And, the smell of the house thinned, as if some molecules had been taken out of the air. Also time slowed down. Sometimes I looked at the clock thinking it'd been a half hour and only five minutes had gone by. It was like my mom's departure had literally altered the physical properties of matter, space, and time.

Mitch lied about the soccer. He never went out for the team, but I didn't blame him. Some of the other stuff was true. I knew what it was like to have a girlfriend because I'd had a couple. The last one was Julie. I spent all my free time trying to figure out if she was really pissed or just faking being pissed, and what I was supposed to do about it. For a long time it was worth it for the sex, but when I stopped caring about that, then what was the point?

I ate some scrambled eggs and shoved some around on my plate.

My dad poured himself his second cup of coffee and put some milk in it. I watched the white milk swirl and mix with the dark coffee.

"I'll drive you to school," he said.

"I'll take the bus."

"I'll drive you to the bus."

"It's two blocks."

"I don't want to leave you alone like this."

"Like what?" I stared at him, but he met my look with his own and I had to look away. That look was full of all kinds of shit I didn't want to face. His love, his grief, his fear of losing his last family member. Why was that my responsibility?

"I'm fine," I said. "I swear to god. I just…I went for a walk and got to thinking about…you know."

"Tell me what you were thinking."

"I just did."

He sort of laughed and stood next to me, put his hand on my shoulder, and squeezed it. "We'll get through this."

"Get through what?"

He removed his hand, sighed. "If you promise me you're not going to hurt yourself...or kill yourself, I'll let you walk to the bus."

"I promise."

"Say it."

I stared down at my hands. Why do they think we won't lie about this? "I promise I won't hurt myself or kill myself."

"I love you. I'll see you tonight." My dad kissed me on the top of the head and left the room.

I heard him leave the house, get into the car, start it up. I went to the living room and peeked through the front window as his blue Chevy sedan drove away.

What my dad didn't know was that I knew about the gun. He'd bought it years before, back when he thought the evil lurked outside the house, that it might break in some night and threaten his family. When he found out the evil was already in our heads—Mom's and mine—he thought he could keep me safe by hiding the gun and the ammo in different places.

Home all summer, I searched the house and garage. I found one key in the bottom right desk drawer and poked it into every keyhole in the house until it found its mate in the metal lockbox tucked beneath a layer of pink insulation in the attic. I found another key under a can of sardines in the pantry and found its mate in a filing cabinet in the garage. A gun in the attic, ammo in the garage—both carefully hidden and securely locked. What were the odds that the two would meet?

As soon as my dad's car was out of sight I went to the den and got the key, then made my way to the attic and retrieved the gun. It was familiar from the hours I'd spent holding it, testing the safety and trigger, even pointing it at my head and feeling the hollow click echo in my skull. How many times had I sat cross-legged on the floor—my heart racing, my palms sweating—and practiced my self-execution? Daring myself to keep my eyes open? Comforted by the weight of the gun in my right hand, the jingle of bullets in my left, knowing that I had the power. I was the alchemist who could bring these two elements together and create peace.

In the garage I found the ammo in the cardboard box behind the files of old tax forms in the bottom drawer. I sat on the floor and opened the box, pulled out six bullets, and began to slide them into the chamber. It seemed important to be thorough, symmetrical.

I heard a car pull into the driveway, a door open and close. It was my dad. He'd tricked me, doubled back to check on me. I finished loading the gun and spun the cylinder like a criminal in a TV cop show, and stuck it to my head. I closed my eyes.

I saw Mitch at McDonalds, flipping his hair out of his face. I saw Julie under me the first time, a mix of fear and trust in her eyes as she let me in. I saw my dad at the funeral reception in his plaid shirt and tie, drowning in a house full of pity. I saw my mom's tired hazel eyes, too tired for her love to get through.

"Justin, put the gun down." It was my dad's voice, nearby.

When I opened my eyes, I saw a dark world blurred by my tears.

"I can't," I said. And it was true, I couldn't pull the gun away, couldn't move. But I also meant something else, something to do with Mitch's lock of hair and my mom's yellow cup and all those trashcans lining the street. I couldn't keep walking the earth with all that sewage flowing and mixing beneath my feet. "I can't," I repeated.

"Just point it at me," my dad said.

Ashes

David Raines

It takes so little to snuff out so great a form. I touched a tiny glowing match to brittle hay and watched the flame take hold like a greedy child grasping at his mother's breast. I stepped back reluctantly, uncertain whether to stop the fire as it patiently reached out, straw by straw, and encircled the barn.

This would not take long.

Twilight had yielded to darkness and the world was in shadow save for the radiating flicker of fire light. It crept up the barn doors, chasing sooty black stains that bled into the dead, gray wood. The autumn air was seasoned with pungent smoke as the barn coughed raspy plumes. Flames burst here and there through splintery planks, as if the façade had suddenly opened angry yellow eyes, glaring at me in furious rebuke. Its smoky cough soon gave way to fiery screams.

Shrouded in black vapor, I stepped farther away, moving upwind to see the blaze reach back along the barn's broad side. I felt the sting of smoke in the back of my throat and coughed out the barn's ashy flesh. I wiped black mucus from my nose and tried to drink in fresh night air.

Tendrils of flame pierced the studded gambrel. Knots of tinder exploded — Pop! Pop! Pop! — shooting ember sparks into the moonless night sky. I heard the rending of rusted iron and the barn doors gave one last howl before crashing into a heap of shattered matchwood teeth. The conflagration blazed along the roofline and I could hear the barn's back breaking as splintery muscle sizzled and rugged bone rafters became brittle and fractured.

Finally, a fireball punched through the back of the barn and the entire structure hemorrhaged fiery blood. I watched its face slide free of its body and collapse in a dead heap. Its back snapped and the entire construction folded in upon itself, billowing arid smoke like a hellish black fog.

I sat silently with the funeral pyre until the sky turned purple with the coming dawn. Until the glowing embers dissolved into nothingness. Until the warm autumn wind began to stir the remains softly along the road and blew dry soil gently over a terrestrial urn. Ashes to dust, dust to ashes.

Whitney Portal

Oriana

What she loved was the view
of the highest peak –
the mountain's two great wings,
a granite angel. Silent strokes

were eroding the trails
in my mother's brain.
I thought, if only she could live
in a nursing home near Lone Pine,

looking at Mt. Whitney –
the mountain she loved, had climbed
on her birthday so many times.
But the dying

leave before the last breath.
She would not have seen the real
Mt. Whitney. Nor did she need
to, my mother, ninety,

in a deepening coma
climbing steep switchbacks
with my father –
Then the gesture, before

all motion stopped:
she lifted her arm and reached
for his hand,
to help her cross the last stream.

Contributors

Scott Barbour is a member and volunteer for San Diego Writers, Ink. He's a regular at Thursday Writers and co-hosts Room to Write on the first and third Sunday of every month. His work has appeared in First Friday CD of Year 3 and *A Year in Ink, Volume 3*.

Gina Barnard has published in *New Madrid, Web Del Sol, Poetry Now, Cosumnes River Review*, and in Japanese translation in *Poemaholic Café* (Tsukuba, Japan). She is currently a contributing editor for Poetry International and will graduate with an MFA from SDSU in Spring 2011. She was born in Fussa, Tokyo, and spent her early years between Japan and the Sacramento Valley, California.

Tina Barton's poetry has appeared in *WestWard Quarterly Magazine, San Diego Writer's, Ink Anthology IV* and the *San Diego Poetry Annual*. A set of eight poems will be featured in the Anthology *Bound by the Secrets We Trust* (Hedcleanr Books, 2011). *San Diego Magazine* and *ConnotationPress.com* have published Barton's short stories.

Linda Boltman has had her stories and poetry published in *Adventures for the Average Woman* in both their magazine, ezine and kindle editions, in *GreenPrints Magazine*, the *San Diego Reader* and other publications. Watch for her new book, *Man in the Moon*, to be released this spring by Jigsaw Press and available at Barnes & Noble and Amazon.com. See http://www.lboltman.blogspot.com.

Janice Coy is an award winning former journalist. Most recently, she received an honorable mention in the 78th Annual *Writer's Digest* Writing Competition. Janice wrote "Almost Gone" for a San Diego DimeStories Open Mic Night. The piece is about her youngest who left soon after for college.

Charlie Daly comes from Boston, Ireland, and more recently, Ocean Beach. He is 21 years old. He has work in: *Grey Sparrow Journal* (Summer 2011), *Shoots and Vines, Troubadour 21, Gloom Cupboard, Writers bloc* (Rutgers), *A Year in Ink III, Steez* and the *Survivor's Review*. Read him at: charliedaly.wordpress.com.

Tracy Darling is an emerging poet, as in she just emerged—mostly intact—from eleven years of staying home to raise her three children. She writes confessional poetry, though she hasn't been to church in years, preferring to run by mass on Sunday mornings instead.

Aurielle Destiche enjoys food, the ballet and caffeinated beverages. Currently, she works as an Associate Editor and is applying to MFA Programs for Fall 2011.

Lindsey Donner is a writer, editor and blogger who runs a design and editorial consultancy called Well Versed Creative with her husband. Born in New Jersey, Lindsey graduated from NYU in 2006. She still can't believe there are so many other East Coasters in San Diego.

Although she spent most of her youth abroad, **Kirsten Francis'** (cover art) childhood was truly spent within the world created by the books she read. Her love for a good story along with an active imagination inspires and informs the woodblock prints she makes, creating a colorful and complex narrative. Her work can be seen at www.kirstenfrancis.com.

Kyra Freeburg is a feature writer in Health & Wellbeing and Philosophy at Flickspin. She just finished writing her third book and has a fourth in progress. Kyra studied at the Iowa Writers workshop. When not writing, she's a Life Coach, Intuitive Counselor and pure genius at instigating fun.

Nickolas Furr is a freelance writer and independent blogger, a former alt-journalist and a proud member of North County Writers of Speculative Fiction. He writes fantasy, reads science fiction and hails from the South. He lives in Imperial Beach with his girl, Liza, and their dog, Adam.

Judy Geraci continues to work on her "Tri-City" short-story collection. Two other stories, "Tri-City" and "Baby, It's You" appeared in previous *A Year in Ink* anthologies. At her current rate of progress, Judy hopes to complete the collection before she collects Social Security. She thanks all who have helped her.

Beth Goldner is the author of *Wake: Stories* and *The Number We End Up With: a Novel,* both published by Basic Books. Her short fiction has appeared in literary journals, including T*he Missouri Review, The Massachusetts Review*, and *Story Quarterly.* She is a recent transplant from Philadelphia, and she does not miss the snow.

L.A. Grove was born amid the dairy farms of Wisconsin and raised under the gray skies of West Michigan. She currently works as a contributing editor for Poetry International. Her work has appeared in *Acappella Zoo, Web Del Sol* and *Pandemonium.* She has poems forthcoming in *Hummingbird Magazine.*

Bridget Hanley has lived in San Diego since 1975. Besides poetry, she also writes prose and creates poetry montage art pieces. She does accounting and various freelance projects for a living. Her website, www.bridgethanley.com, displays more of her writing and montages.

Michael Hemmingson's collection of poems, *Ourselves or Nothing,* was published last year by Olympia Press. His poetry has appeared in a number of print and online journals.

Pete Hepburn is retired. His poetry and prose publications include: *The Acorn, The Gnu, The Boston Literary Review, The Houston Literary Review, San Diego Poetry Annual, San Diego Writers Ink Anthology,* Dime Stories CDs, and *San Diego CityBeat.* He is currently batting .666 in the La Mesa Senior Softball League.

Randy Herman is Ryan, Tad and Chapin's dad. He is also a recovering actor and a Marriage and Family Therapist. Between offbeat writing challenges and imaginary pick-up football games, he dreams of living in a forested cottage in Del Mar.

Justin Hudnall graduated from New York University's Tisch School of the Arts by way of the Department of Dramatic Writing. He currently acts as Executive Director of So Say We All as well as one of its original founders, and is shopping about his first novel, *Disaster Party.*

Larry Kuechlin lives in Ocean Beach, California. He is the author of *Mountain Biking Orange County* (Globe Pequot Press, 1996), *Along a Ruined Sea* (d/e/a/d/b/e/a/t Publishing, 2008), *Along a Ruined Sea: Special Edition* (Avalon Press, 2009) and *Entrances* (Avalon Press, 2010).

Meredith Kunsa is a native Californian who received her advanced degrees (MPA in Publication Administration and MFA in Creative Writing) from San Diego State University. Her poems have appeared in the *Crab Orchard Review*, *Connecticut Review*, *Los Angeles Review*, *Tiferet*, *Kalliope*, *Silk Road*, *Passager* and *City Works*, among others.

Erik Martin is a newcomer to California and proud to be a member of San Diego Writers, Ink. A Cleveland native, he has been a social worker, bookstore owner and police officer, among other things. "June Gloom & Golden Sand" is only his second published story.

Seretta Martin is a regional editor of San Diego Poetry Annual, and serves on the editorial staff of Poetry International Journal. At Barnes & Noble, Grossmont Center, she hosts the 3rd Wednesday poetry series. She finds joy in teaching poetry and the Border Voices Poetry Project. Her writing is well published in journals such as *A Year in Ink*, Web del Sol and Margi. Her book, *Foreign Dust, Familiar Rain* is available on barnesandnoble.com. Seretta welcomes your correspondence at wordsoup@juno.com

Patrick McMahon is a San Diego writer, photographer and musician. The piece in this anthology is excerpted from his memoir, a sensitive exploration of identity by means of re-connecting with blood relatives after growing up adopted. Look for *Becoming Patrick* in the Spring 2011. He can be contacted at www.patrickmc.com.

Melissa Milazzo spends her days as an editor for scientific publishing company. Her fiction has appeared in several online venues. She lives in Normal Heights with her husband and a ridiculous dog.

Originally from the San Francisco Bay Area, **Carrie Moniz** currently resides in San Diego, California. Her poems have appeared or are forthcoming in *Transform This*, *Yellow Medicine Review*, Third Wednesday, *Suisun Valley Review* and *an island of egrets* Haiku Anthology.

Una Nichols Hynum born Providence RI. Graduate of SDSU and finalist for James Hearst Poetry Prize, Margie and Writers Digest, nominated for the Pushcart , member of the Squaw Valley Community of Writers, published in *Spillway, Rattle, an island of egrets* and, best of all, *A Year in Ink.*

A former journalist and college instructor, **Oriana** was born in Poland and came to the United States when she was 17. Her poems, essays and translations have been published in *Poetry, Ploughshares, Best American Poetry 1992, Nimrod, New Letters, The Iowa Review, American Poetry Review, Prairie Schooner, Southern Poetry Review* and many other magazines and anthologies.

Cris Powell practices psychotherapy and contemporary psychoanalysis in San Diego, and consults internationally via webcam. She is a Training and Supervising Analyst for the Institute of Contemporary Psychoanalysis in Los Angeles. Her forthcoming memoir, *Emotional Orphans*, tells the stories of traumatized children and adolescents and how they healed themselves.

Mark Radoff is a writer from North County. If irreverence was a currency he'd be entitled to a tax cut. Florentino is his first published piece. He is currently working on a novel about Northwest New Mexico, the harmonic convergence, Gnostics, chicken franchises, William McKinley, uranium mining, Anasazi pottery, religious imperialism and checkerboards.

David Raines is a writer/photographer living in San Diego. He has written for *North Park News, San Diego Metropolitan, The Daily Aztec* and *San Diego Magazine.* This is his first story for the *San Diego Writers, Ink Anthology.* You can view his other work at www.rainestorm.com.

After graduating from SDCC with a degree in Electronics, **Dave Riessen** changed his major to English and focused on creative writing at SDSU.

Sandy Robertson lived in China and Japan as a child. She came to San Diego to pursue graduate study and has made her home here ever since. A former teacher and a life-long lover of language, her other publications are in the field of Spanish literature and film.

Sharon Rosen Leib is an occasional poet and a frequent mother of three daughters. She writes the column "Musings From Mama" for the *San Diego Jewish Journal*. A proud 4th generation Californian, she contributed to NPR's "California Dreaming" series and is writing a book about her family's Hollywood movie-biz history.

Shawna A. Smart is the author of several published short stories, sprinkled along her life path like solitary starfish over the past 15 years. She lives in San Diego with her partner, Andy, and two very spoiled cats.

Janet Tait lives in San Diego, CA with her husband. Before wholeheartedly embracing the life of a writer she rejected careers as an administrative assistant, webmaster, IT manager and competitive intelligence specialist. Her fiction and non-fiction has been published in *Thaumatrope*, *Tweet the Meat, Cerise* and *GeniusHour Magazine*.

David W. Tuffy serves as President of The Board for the nonprofit So Say We All: a San Diego local literary, performing and visual arts advocacy and production group. He occasionally writes and performs for their monthly show VAMP. David lives in a small apartment in North Park with no cats.

Nicole Vollrath earned her MFA in Creative Writing at Emerson College in Boston. She served as prose editor for the literary journal *Beacon Street Review*, director of Phone-A-Poem, and as a reader for *Ploughshares* and *Agni*. She regularly teaches at UCSD Extention, and co-hosts Room to Write at San Diego Writers, Ink.

Angie Vorhies is a poet, translator, photographer, food writer and co-founder of San Diego Roots Sustainable Food Project. She lives in South Park with her daughters, Tyler, Kelsey and Siena.

Kenneth Zak is a novelist and poet residing in San Diego, California. His debut manuscript, *The Poet's Secret*, was a 2010 RWA Golden Heart finalist. Visit him at www.kennethzak.com or on Facebook at Kenneth Zak (San Diego).

Monika Zobel was raised in Northern Germany and has been living in the U.S. since 2001. She is a contributing editor at Poetry International. Her poems have appeared online at *Counterexample Poetics*, in *Best New Poets 2010*, and are forthcoming in *Zoland Poetry* and *Blue Moon Literary & Art Review*.

Editors

Jericho Brown worked as the speechwriter for the Mayor of New Orleans before receiving his PhD in Creative Writing and Literature from the University of Houston. He also holds an MFA from the University of New Orleans and a BA from Dillard University. The recipient of the Whiting Writers Award and fellowships from the National Endowment for the Arts, the Radcliffe Institute at Harvard University, the Bread Loaf Writers' Conference, and the Krakow

Poetry Seminar in Poland, Brown is an Assistant Professor at the University of San Diego. His poems have appeared in journals and anthologies including, The Iowa Review, jubilat, Oxford American, Ploughshares, A Public Space, and 100 Best African American Poems. His first book, *Please* (New Issues), won the American Book Award.

Laurel Corona has combined her love of writing and teaching for more than three decades. She has taught in the San Diego area since 1975, working first at SDSU then at UCSD, and is currently a professor of Humanities at San Diego City College. She began her career as a published author in 1999 with a book on Kenya for Lucent Books, and went on to write seventeen Young Adult titles for that company before turning her attention to books for adults. In 2008 she had award-winning debuts with major publishers in both fiction and non-fiction. *The Four Seasons: A Novel of Vivaldi's Venice*

(Hyperion/VOICE 2008) won the 2009 Theodor Geisel Award for Book of the Year from the San Diego Book Awards and has been translated into eleven foreign languages. *Until Our Last Breath: A Holocaust Story of Love and Partisan Resistance* (St. Martin's Press 2008) is a non-fiction work about the Jewish resistance movement in Vilna, Lithuania.

It won a San Diego Book Award as well as a Christopher Medal, a national award given to books whose writers "craft words and images into a clear, cohesive vision" and "affirm the highest values of the human spirit." Corona's second novel, *Penelope's Daughter* (Penguin/Berkley 2010), tells the story of Homer's Odyssey from the perspective of a daughter born to Odysseus after he leaves for Troy. Her third novel, *The Laws of Motion* (Simon and Schuster/Gallery 2011) is based on the life story of Emilie du Chatelet, the brilliant eighteenth-century physicist and mathematician who was also Voltaire's lover and muse. She is currently at work on her fourth novel, set in Spain at the time of Ferdinand and Isabella.

San Diego Writers, Ink is a nonprofit literary organization that nurtures writers and those wishing to explore the craft of writing, fosters a literary community, promotes literature and celebrates artistic diversity.

The Ink Spot, located in the Art Center Lofts in San Diego's East Village, is our gathering place where we offer classes, groups, workshops, readings, and other literary events. The Ink Spot is also home to the Arts Council Gallery, which features the work of local artists.

SDW, Ink collaborates with other artistic, cultural, and community organizations throughout the city and county to promote literature and to inspire the community of writers.

We are grateful to The Merci Fund at the San Diego Foundation for its generous support and to Kirsten Francis for her generosity.

San Diego Writers, Ink
P.O. Box 34374
San Diego, CA 92163

The Ink Spot
710 13th St., Studio 210
San Diego, CA 92101

www.sandiegowriters.org

Order additional copies of *A Year in Ink, Volume 1* (2008), edited by Thomas Larson; *Volume 2* (2009), edited by Sandra Alcosser and Arthur Salm; *Volume 3* (2010), edited by Roger Aplon and Jennifer Silva Redmond; and *Volume 4* (2011), edited by Jericho Brown and Laurel Corona at our website.

www.ingramcontent.com/pod-product-compliance
Lightning Source LLC
Chambersburg PA
CBHW060121260626
47160CB00005B/1967